Yannick Grotholt – Writer

Comicon – Artist

PAPERCUT Z™

New York

LEGO CHIMA Graphic Novels Available from PAPERCUTZ

LEGO
LEGENDS OF CHIMA
ALL-NEW GRAPHIC NOVEL SERIES!
HIGH RISK!
PAPERCUTZ

Graphic Novel #1
"High Risk!"

Coming Soon!

LEGO
LEGENDS OF CHIMA
THE RIGHT DECISION
PAPERCUTZ

Graphic Novel #2
"The Right Decision"

Coming Soon!

LEGO
LEGENDS OF CHIMA
YANNICK GROTHOLT
COMICON
PAPERCUTZ

Graphic Novel #3

FSC
www.fsc.org
MIX
Paper from responsible sources
FSC® C016245

LEGO LEGENDS OF CHIMA graphic novels are available for $7.99 in paperback, $12.99 hardcover. Available from booksellers everywhere. You can also order online from Papercutz.com. Or call 1-800-886-1223, Monday through Friday, 9-5 EST. MC, Visa, and AmEx accepted. To order by mail, please add $4.00 for postage and handling for first book ordered, $1.00 for each additional book and make check payable to NBM Publishing. Send to: Papercutz, 160 Broadway, Suite 700, East Wing, New York, NY 10039.

LEGO LEGENDS OF CHIMA graphic novels are also available digitally wherever e-books are sold.

Papercutz.com

LEGENDS OF CHIMA
#1 "High Risk!"

Yannick Grotholt – Writer
Comicon – Artist
Tom Orzechowski – Letterer
Max Gartman – Editorial Intern
Beth Scorzato – Production Coordinator
Michael Petranek – Editor
Jim Salicrup
Editor-in-Chief

ISBN: 978-1-62991-072-7 paperback edition
ISBN: 978-1-62991-073-4 hardcover edition

Printed in Canada
April 2014 by Friesens Printing
1 Printer Way
Altona, MB R0G 0B0

Papercutz books may be purchased for business or promotional use. For information on bulk purchases please contact Macmillan Corporate and Premium Sales Department at (800) 221-7945 x5442.

Distributed by Macmillan
First Papercutz Printing

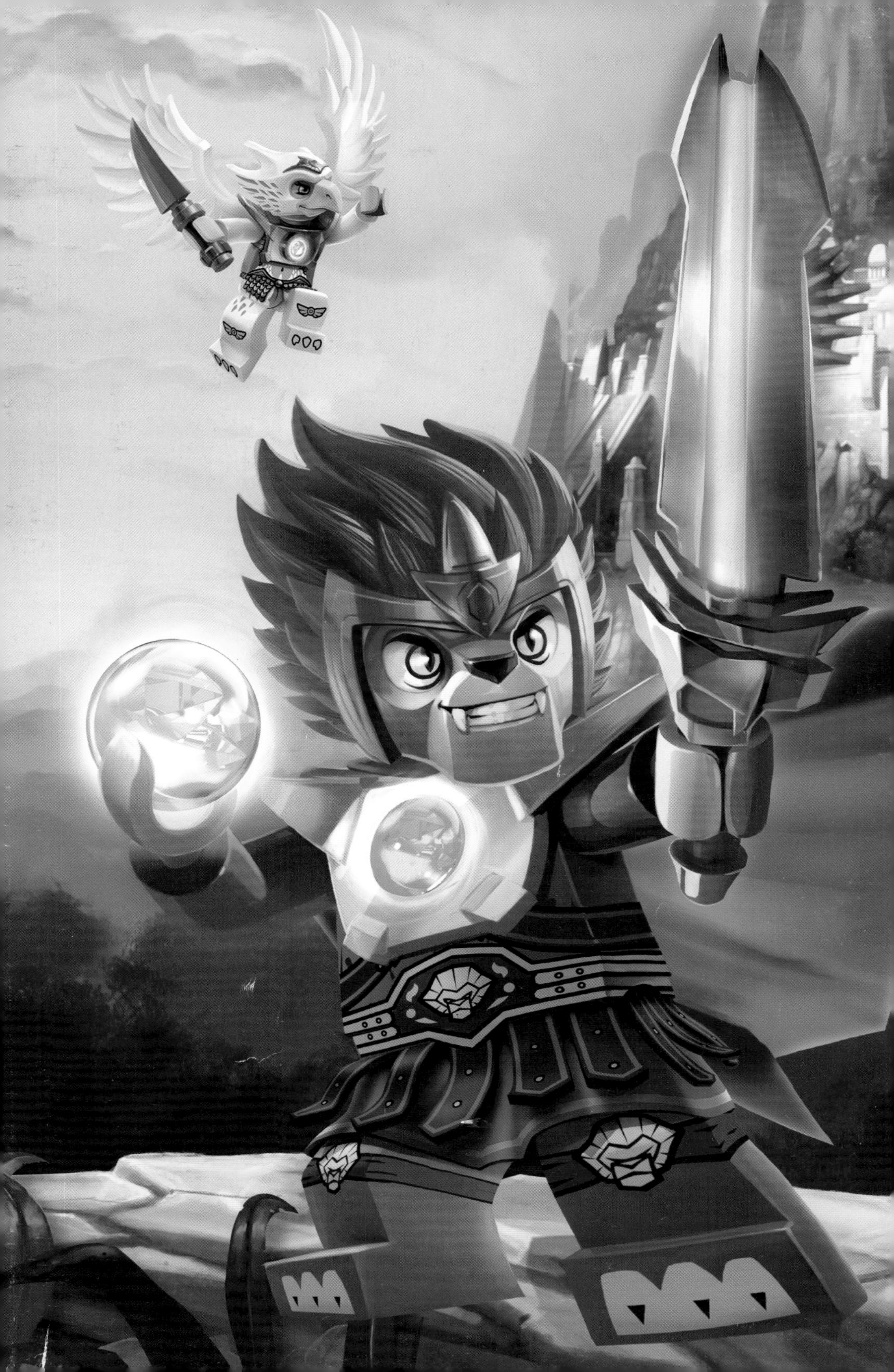

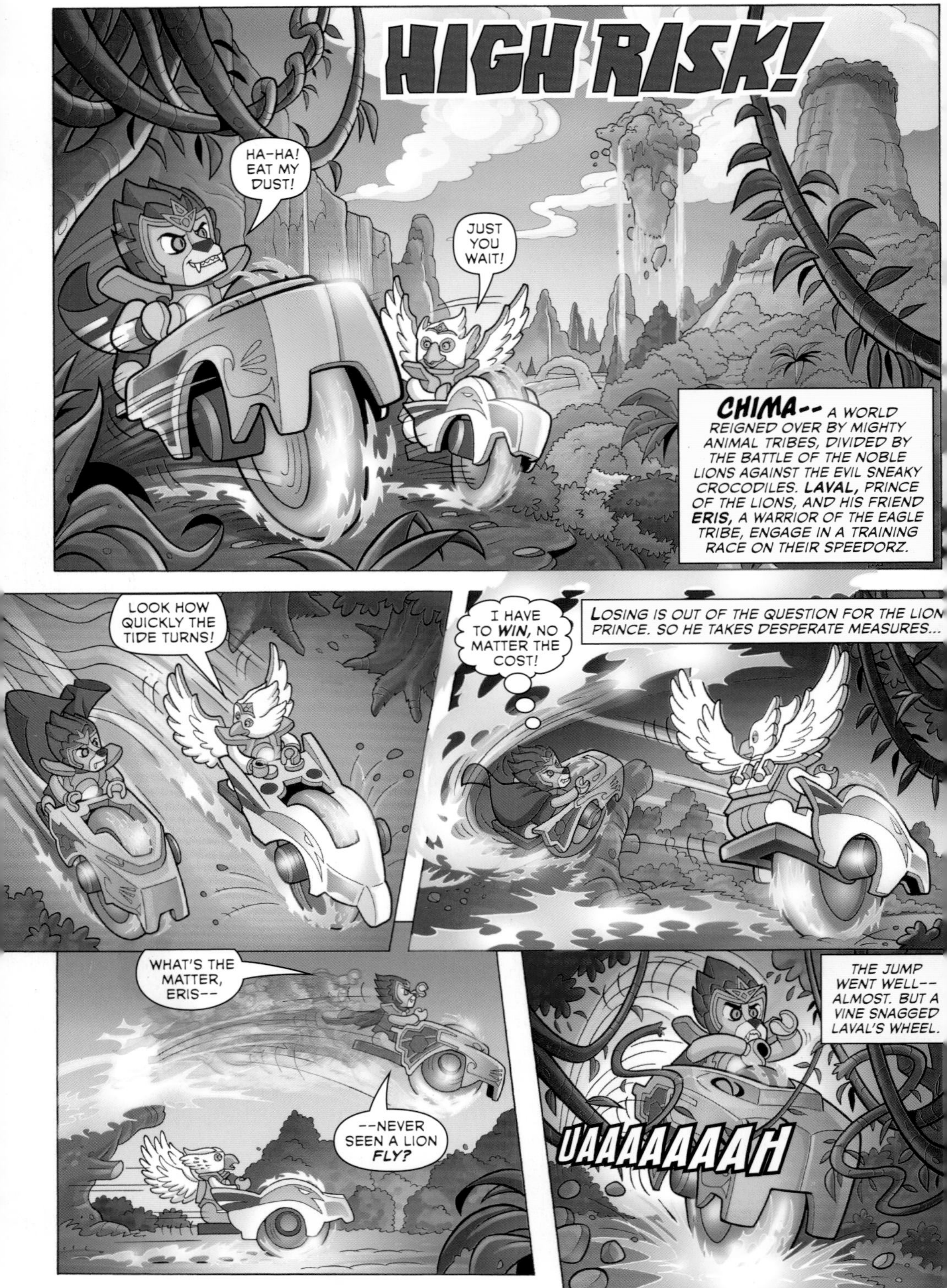
HIGH RISK!
HA-HA! EAT MY DUST!
JUST YOU WAIT!
CHIMA-- A WORLD REIGNED OVER BY MIGHTY ANIMAL TRIBES, DIVIDED BY THE BATTLE OF THE NOBLE LIONS AGAINST THE EVIL SNEAKY CROCODILES. LAVAL, PRINCE OF THE LIONS, AND HIS FRIEND ERIS, A WARRIOR OF THE EAGLE TRIBE, ENGAGE IN A TRAINING RACE ON THEIR SPEEDORZ.
LOOK HOW QUICKLY THE TIDE TURNS!
LOSING IS OUT OF THE QUESTION FOR THE LION PRINCE. SO HE TAKES DESPERATE MEASURES...
I HAVE TO WIN, NO MATTER THE COST!
WHAT'S THE MATTER, ERIS--
--NEVER SEEN A LION FLY?
THE JUMP WENT WELL-- ALMOST. BUT A VINE SNAGGED LAVAL'S WHEEL.
UAAAAAAAAH

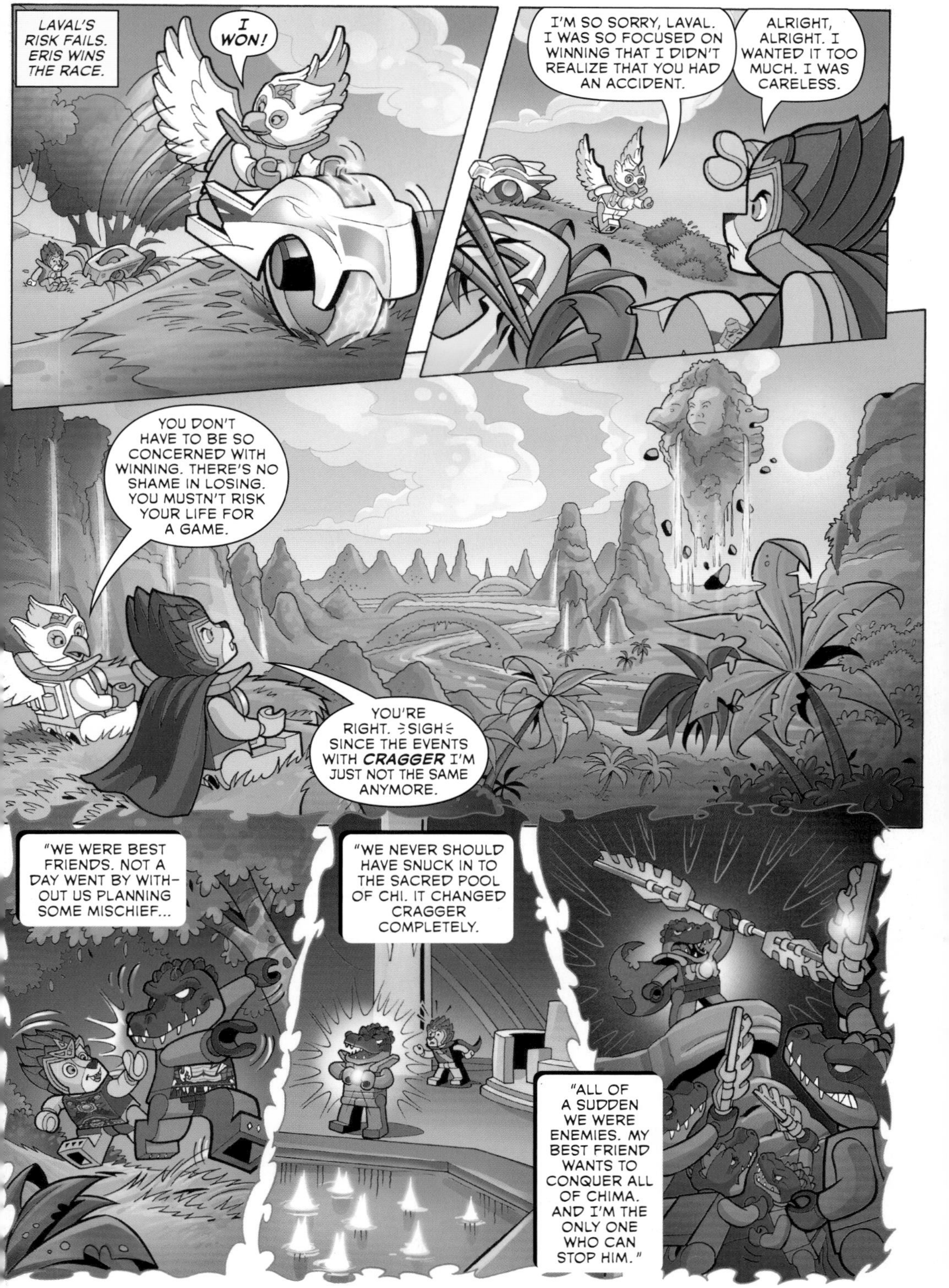
LAVAL'S RISK FAILS. ERIS WINS THE RACE.
I WON!
I'M SO SORRY, LAVAL. I WAS SO FOCUSED ON WINNING THAT I DIDN'T REALIZE THAT YOU HAD AN ACCIDENT.
ALRIGHT, ALRIGHT. I WANTED IT TOO MUCH. I WAS CARELESS.
YOU DON'T HAVE TO BE SO CONCERNED WITH WINNING. THERE'S NO SHAME IN LOSING. YOU MUSTN'T RISK YOUR LIFE FOR A GAME.
YOU'RE RIGHT. ⋛SIGH⋚ SINCE THE EVENTS WITH **CRAGGER** I'M JUST NOT THE SAME ANYMORE.
"WE WERE BEST FRIENDS. NOT A DAY WENT BY WITH-OUT US PLANNING SOME MISCHIEF...
"WE NEVER SHOULD HAVE SNUCK IN TO THE SACRED POOL OF CHI. IT CHANGED CRAGGER COMPLETELY.
"ALL OF A SUDDEN WE WERE ENEMIES. MY BEST FRIEND WANTS TO CONQUER ALL OF CHIMA. AND I'M THE ONLY ONE WHO CAN STOP HIM."

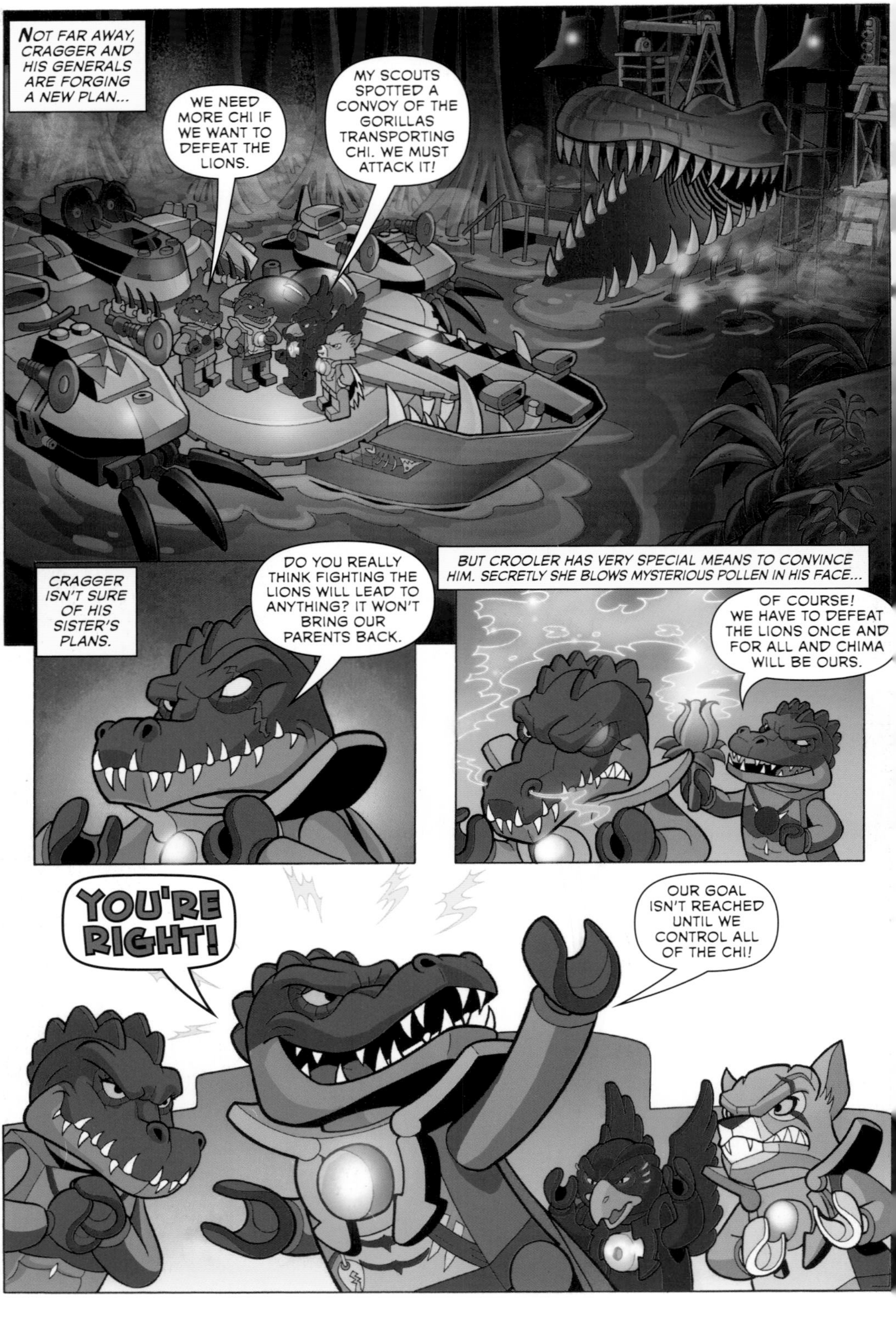

NOT FAR AWAY, CRAGGER AND HIS GENERALS ARE FORGING A NEW PLAN...
WE NEED MORE CHI IF WE WANT TO DEFEAT THE LIONS.
MY SCOUTS SPOTTED A CONVOY OF THE GORILLAS TRANSPORTING CHI. WE MUST ATTACK IT!
CRAGGER ISN'T SURE OF HIS SISTER'S PLANS.
DO YOU REALLY THINK FIGHTING THE LIONS WILL LEAD TO ANYTHING? IT WON'T BRING OUR PARENTS BACK.
BUT CROOLER HAS VERY SPECIAL MEANS TO CONVINCE HIM. SECRETLY SHE BLOWS MYSTERIOUS POLLEN IN HIS FACE...
OF COURSE! WE HAVE TO DEFEAT THE LIONS ONCE AND FOR ALL AND CHIMA WILL BE OURS.
YOU'RE RIGHT!
OUR GOAL ISN'T REACHED UNTIL WE CONTROL ALL OF THE CHI!

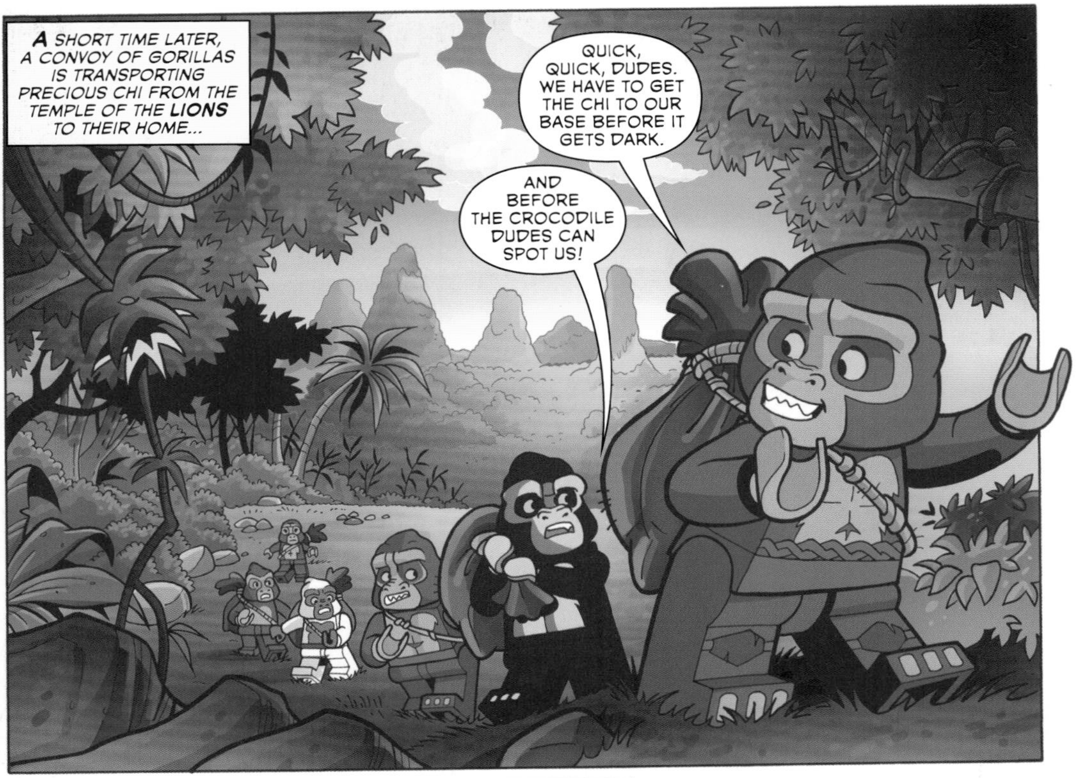
A SHORT TIME LATER, A CONVOY OF GORILLAS IS TRANSPORTING PRECIOUS CHI FROM THE TEMPLE OF THE LIONS TO THEIR HOME...
QUICK, QUICK, DUDES. WE HAVE TO GET THE CHI TO OUR BASE BEFORE IT GETS DARK.
AND BEFORE THE CROCODILE DUDES CAN SPOT US!

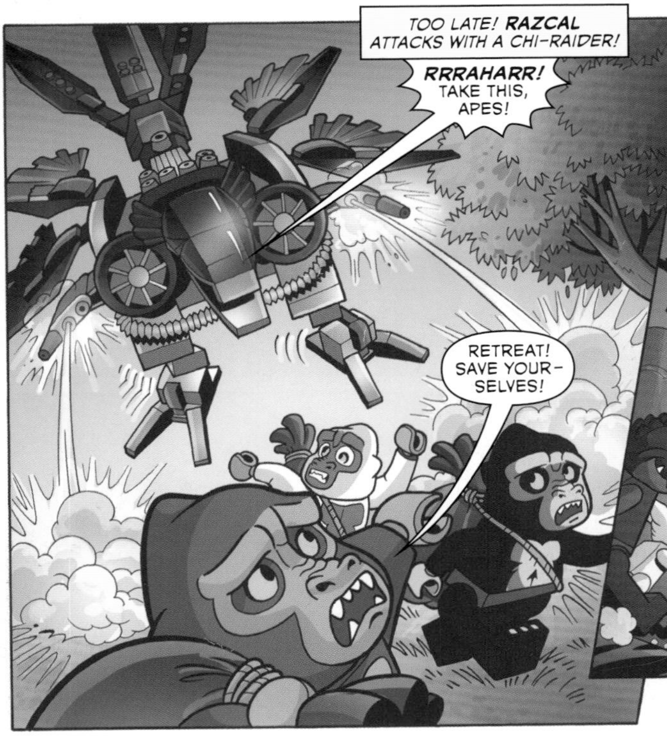
TOO LATE! RAZCAL ATTACKS WITH A CHI-RAIDER!
RRRAHARR! TAKE THIS, APES!
RETREAT! SAVE YOUR-SELVES!

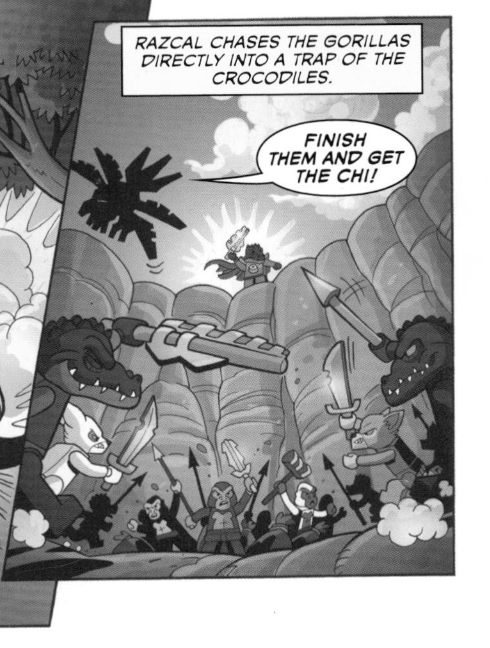
RAZCAL CHASES THE GORILLAS DIRECTLY INTO A TRAP OF THE CROCODILES.
FINISH THEM AND GET THE CHI!

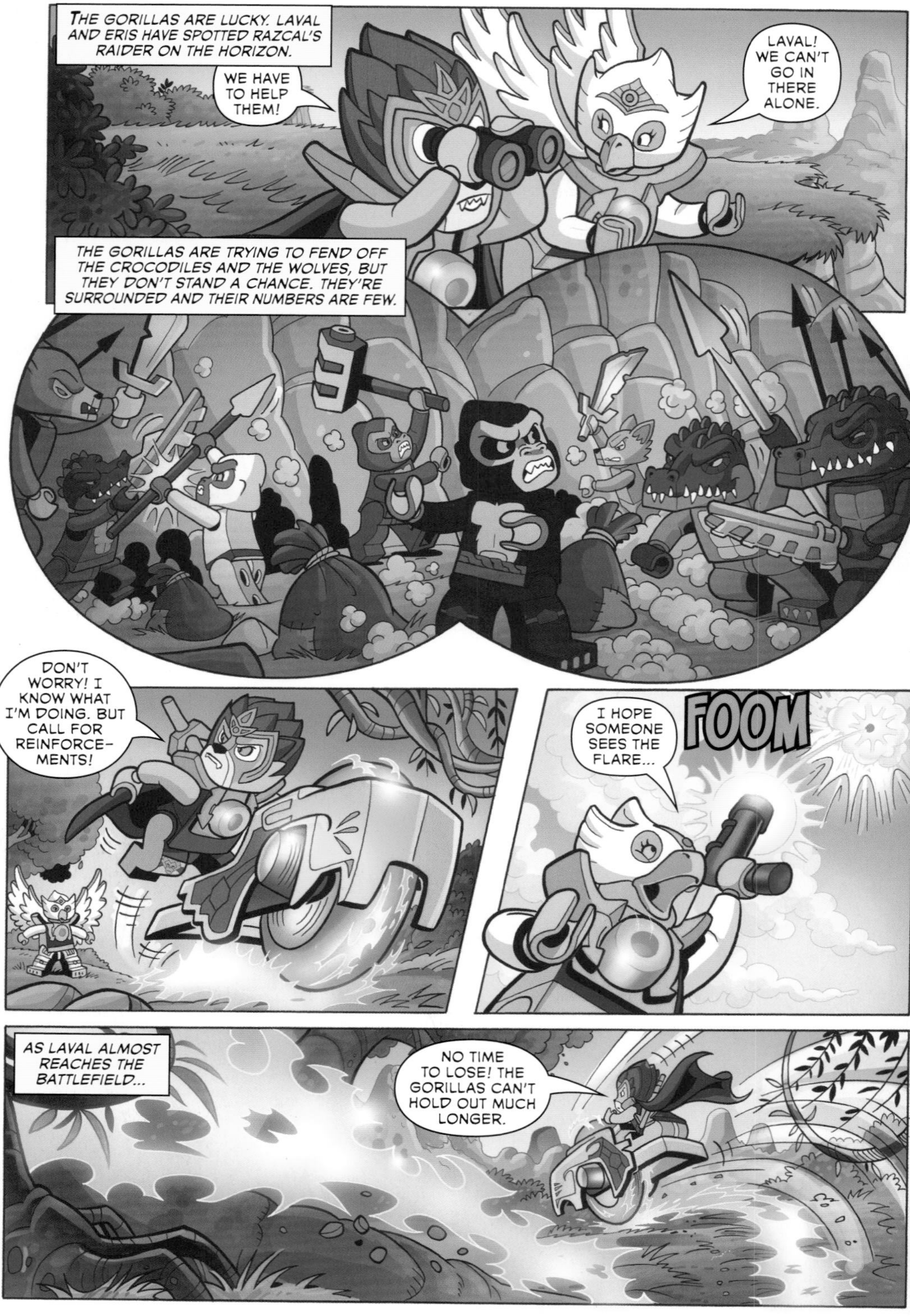
THE GORILLAS ARE LUCKY. LAVAL AND ERIS HAVE SPOTTED RAZCAL'S RAIDER ON THE HORIZON.
WE HAVE TO HELP THEM!
LAVAL! WE CAN'T GO IN THERE ALONE.
THE GORILLAS ARE TRYING TO FEND OFF THE CROCODILES AND THE WOLVES, BUT THEY DON'T STAND A CHANCE. THEY'RE SURROUNDED AND THEIR NUMBERS ARE FEW.
DON'T WORRY! I KNOW WHAT I'M DOING. BUT CALL FOR REINFORCE-MENTS!
I HOPE SOMEONE SEES THE FLARE...
FOOM
AS LAVAL ALMOST REACHES THE BATTLEFIELD...
NO TIME TO LOSE! THE GORILLAS CAN'T HOLD OUT MUCH LONGER.

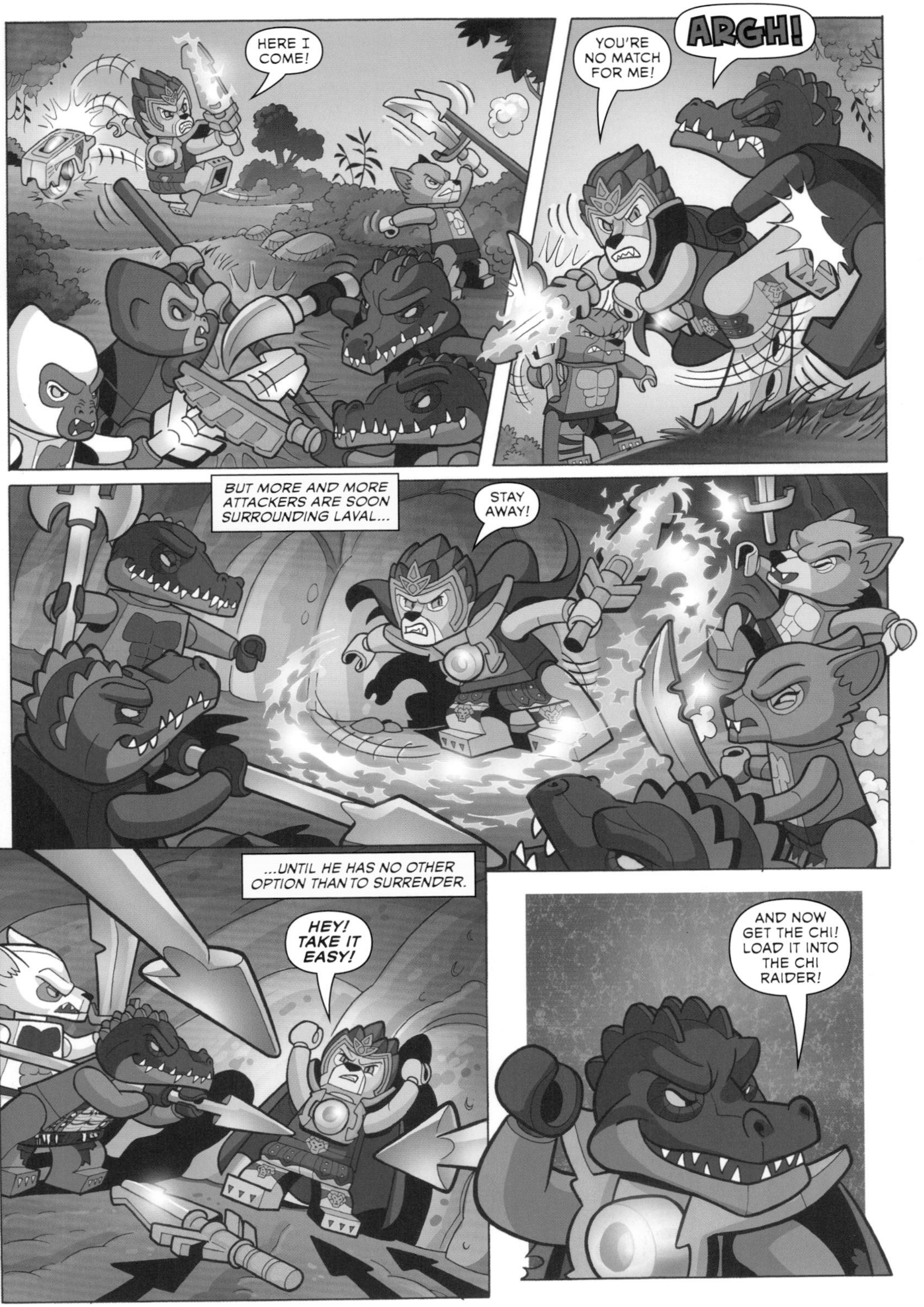
HERE I COME!
YOU'RE NO MATCH FOR ME!
ARGH!
BUT MORE AND MORE ATTACKERS ARE SOON SURROUNDING LAVAL...
STAY AWAY!
...UNTIL HE HAS NO OTHER OPTION THAN TO SURRENDER.
HEY! TAKE IT EASY!
AND NOW GET THE CHI! LOAD IT INTO THE CHI RAIDER!

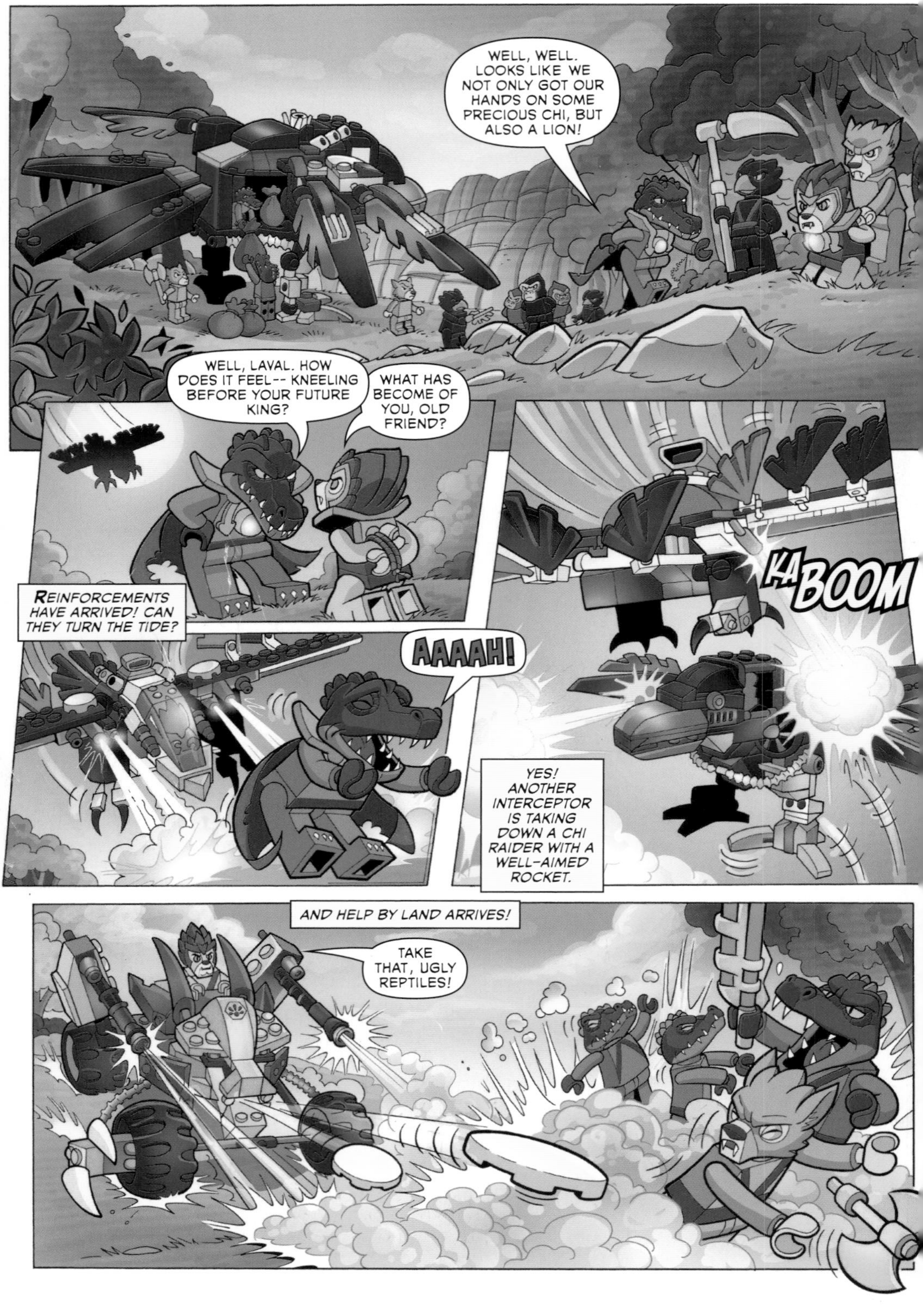
WELL, WELL. LOOKS LIKE WE NOT ONLY GOT OUR HANDS ON SOME PRECIOUS CHI, BUT ALSO A LION!
WELL, LAVAL. HOW DOES IT FEEL-- KNEELING BEFORE YOUR FUTURE KING?
WHAT HAS BECOME OF YOU, OLD FRIEND?
REINFORCEMENTS HAVE ARRIVED! CAN THEY TURN THE TIDE?
AAAAH!
KABOOM
YES! ANOTHER INTERCEPTOR IS TAKING DOWN A CHI RAIDER WITH A WELL-AIMED ROCKET.
AND HELP BY LAND ARRIVES!
TAKE THAT, UGLY REPTILES!

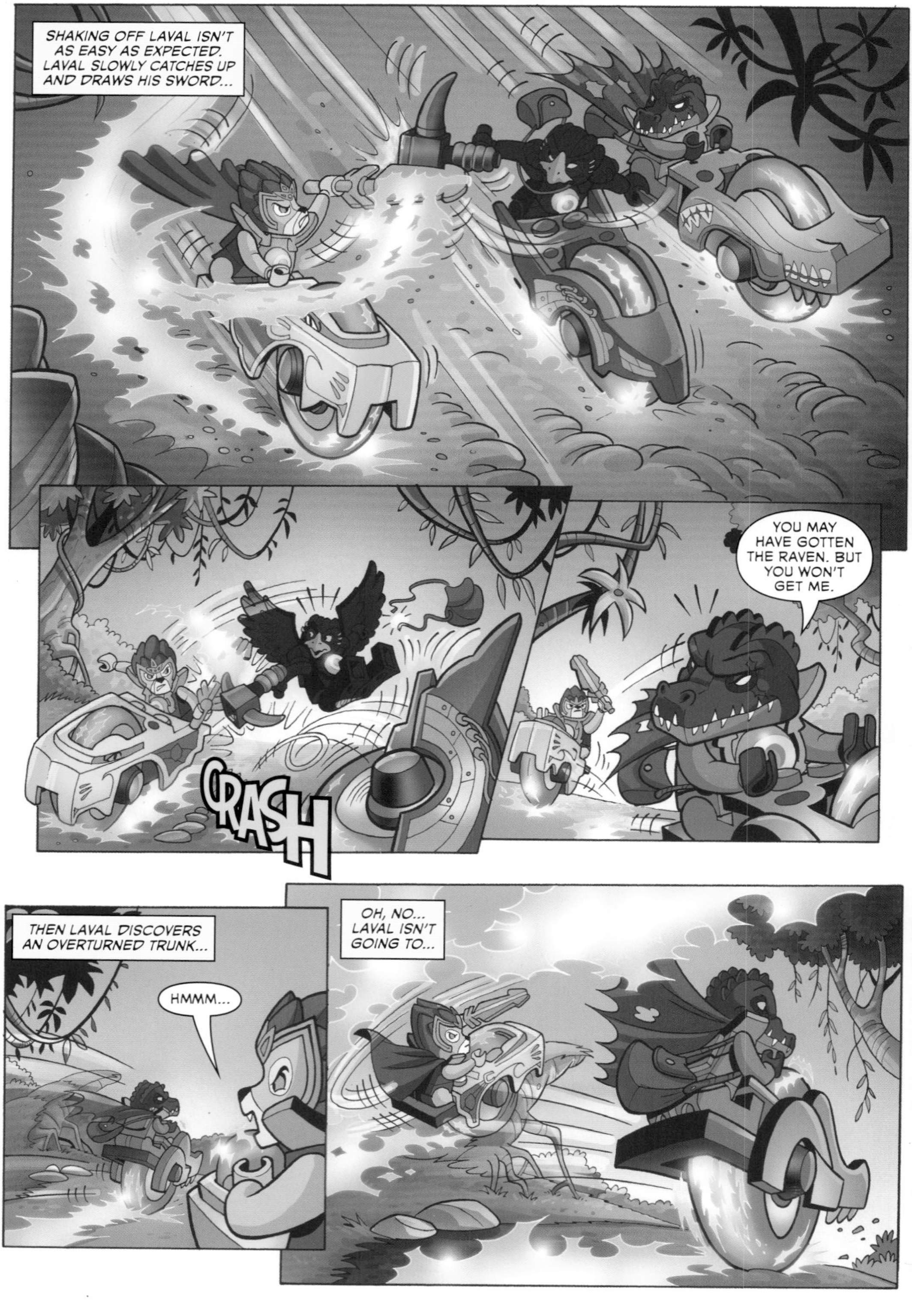
SHAKING OFF LAVAL ISN'T AS EASY AS EXPECTED. LAVAL SLOWLY CATCHES UP AND DRAWS HIS SWORD...
YOU MAY HAVE GOTTEN THE RAVEN. BUT YOU WON'T GET ME.
CRASH
THEN LAVAL DISCOVERS AN OVERTURNED TRUNK...
HMMM...
OH, NO... LAVAL ISN'T GOING TO...

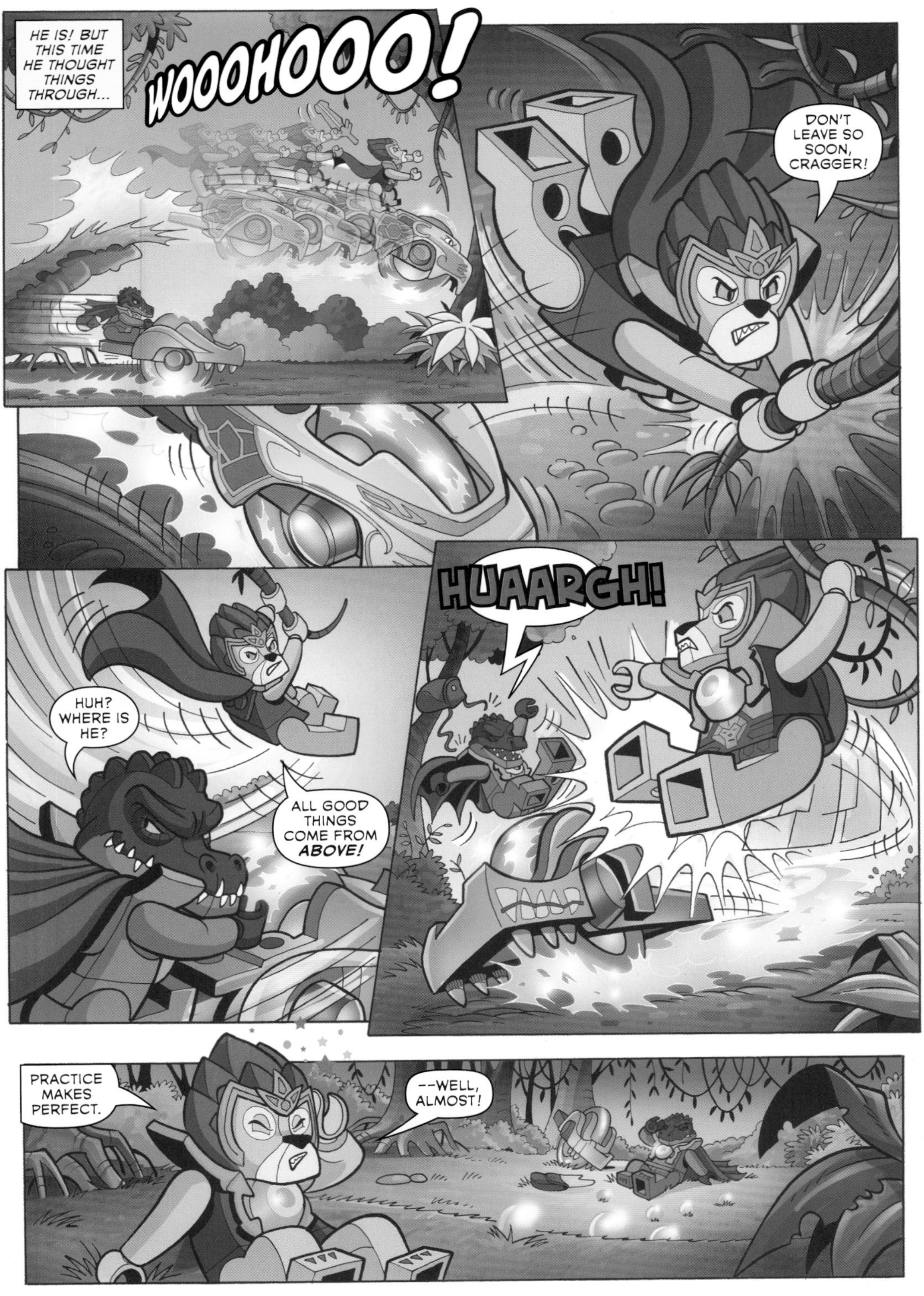
HE IS! BUT THIS TIME HE THOUGHT THINGS THROUGH...
WOOOHOOO!
DON'T LEAVE SO SOON, CRAGGER!
HUH? WHERE IS HE?
ALL GOOD THINGS COME FROM ABOVE!
HUAARGH!
PRACTICE MAKES PERFECT.
--WELL, ALMOST!

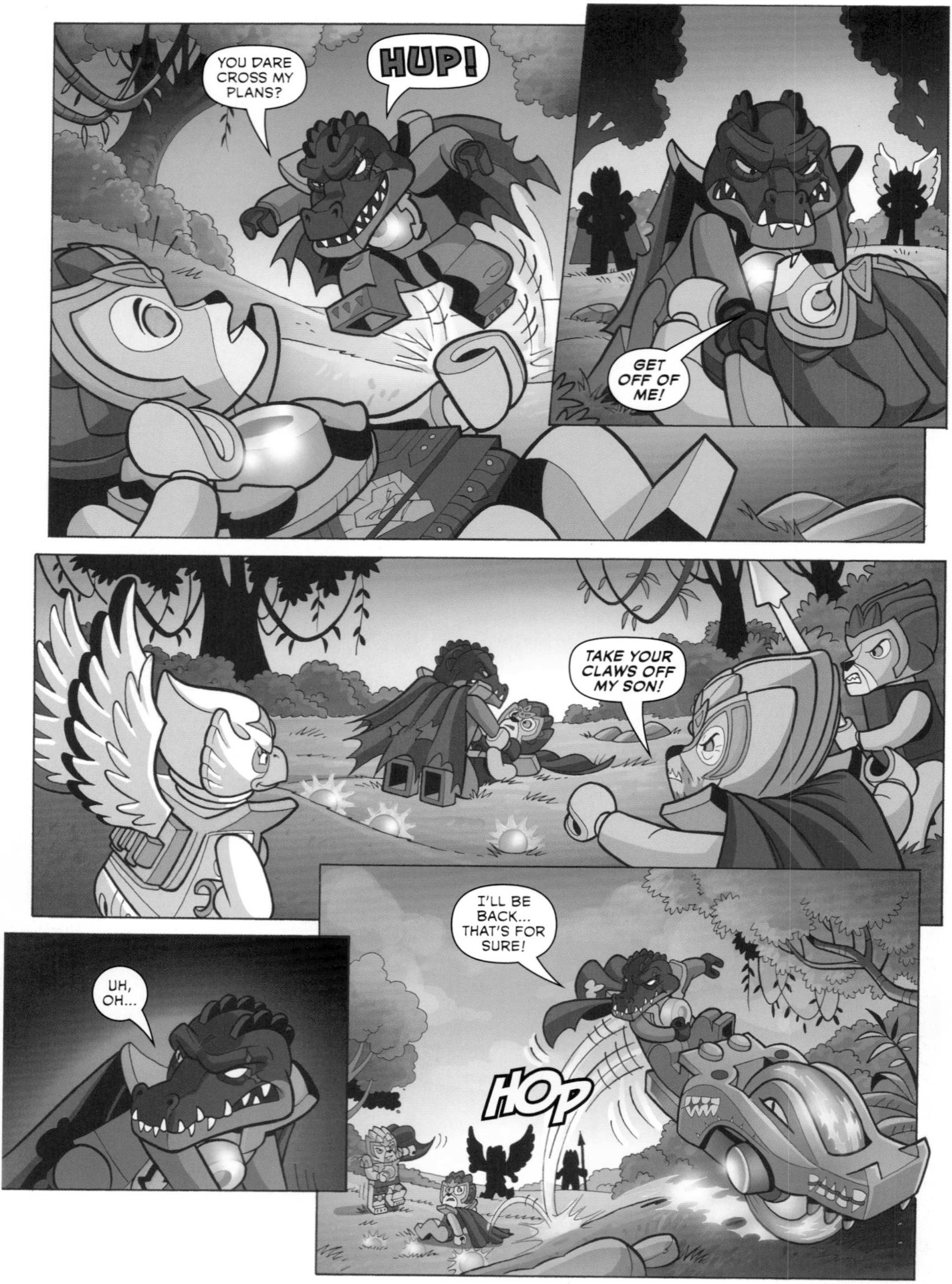
YOU DARE CROSS MY PLANS?
HUP!
GET OFF OF ME!
TAKE YOUR CLAWS OFF MY SON!
UH, OH...
I'LL BE BACK... THAT'S FOR SURE!
HOP

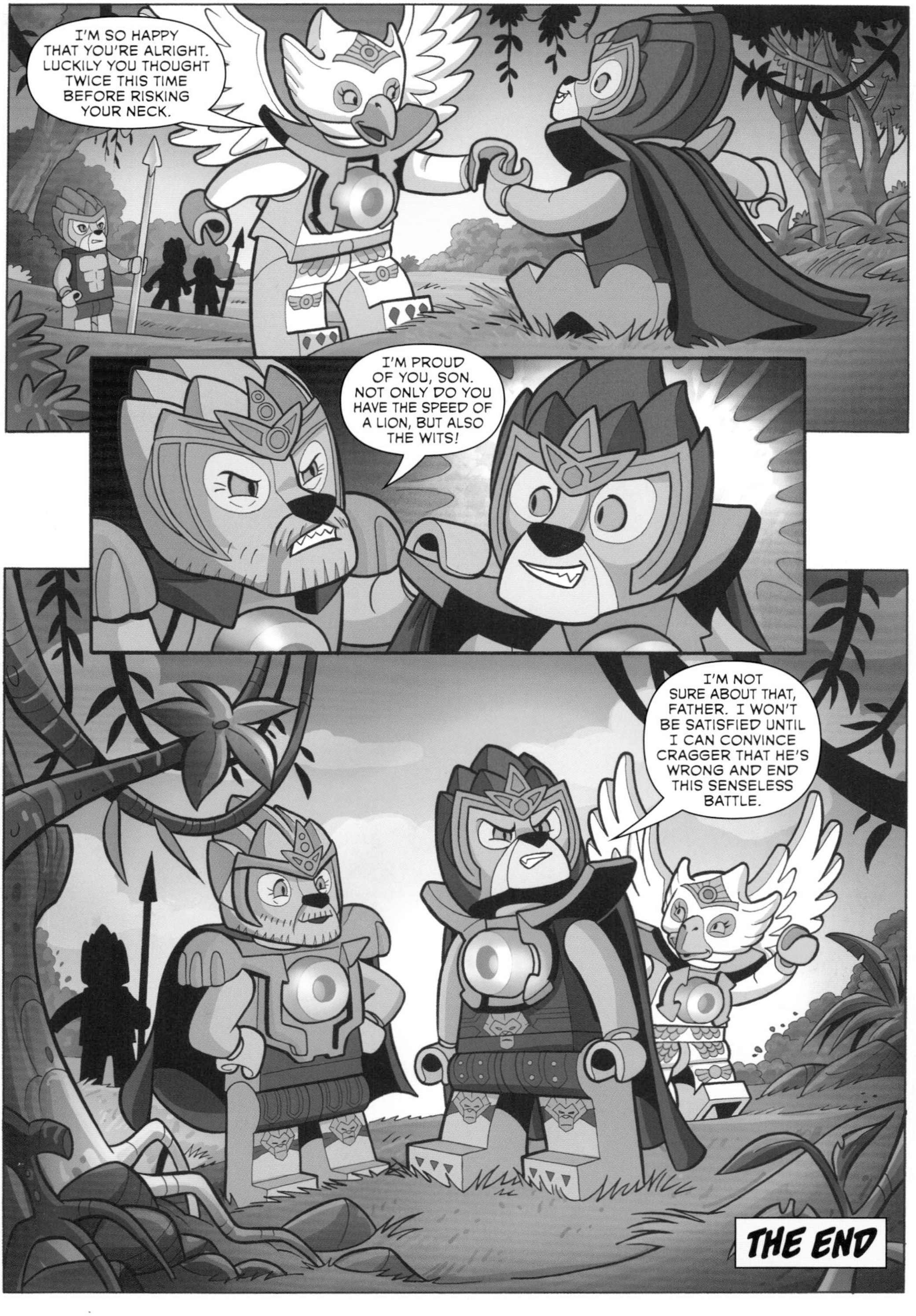
I'M SO HAPPY THAT YOU'RE ALRIGHT. LUCKILY YOU THOUGHT TWICE THIS TIME BEFORE RISKING YOUR NECK.
I'M PROUD OF YOU, SON. NOT ONLY DO YOU HAVE THE SPEED OF A LION, BUT ALSO THE WITS!
I'M NOT SURE ABOUT THAT, FATHER. I WON'T BE SATISFIED UNTIL I CAN CONVINCE CRAGGER THAT HE'S WRONG AND END THIS SENSELESS BATTLE.
THE END

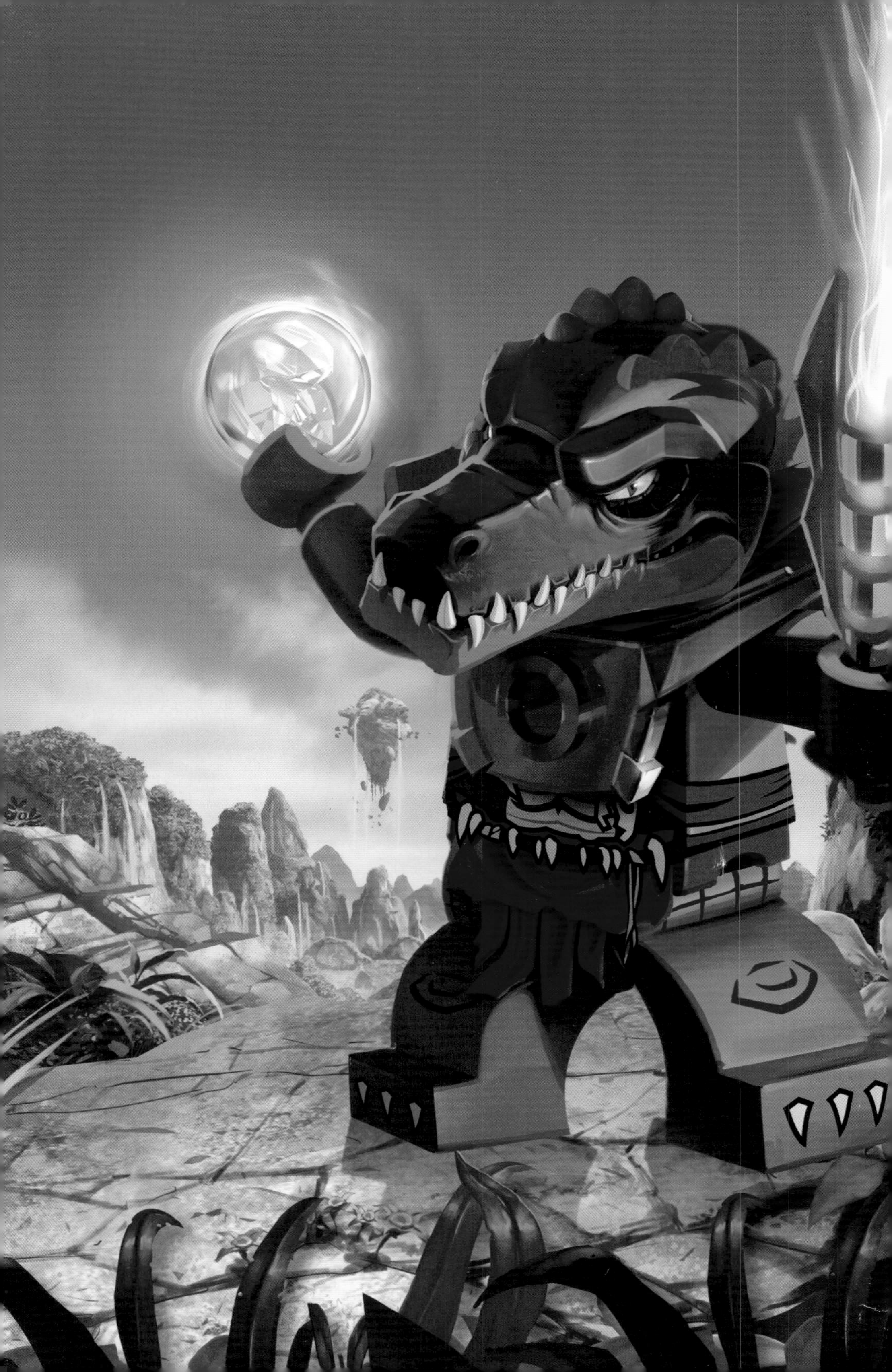

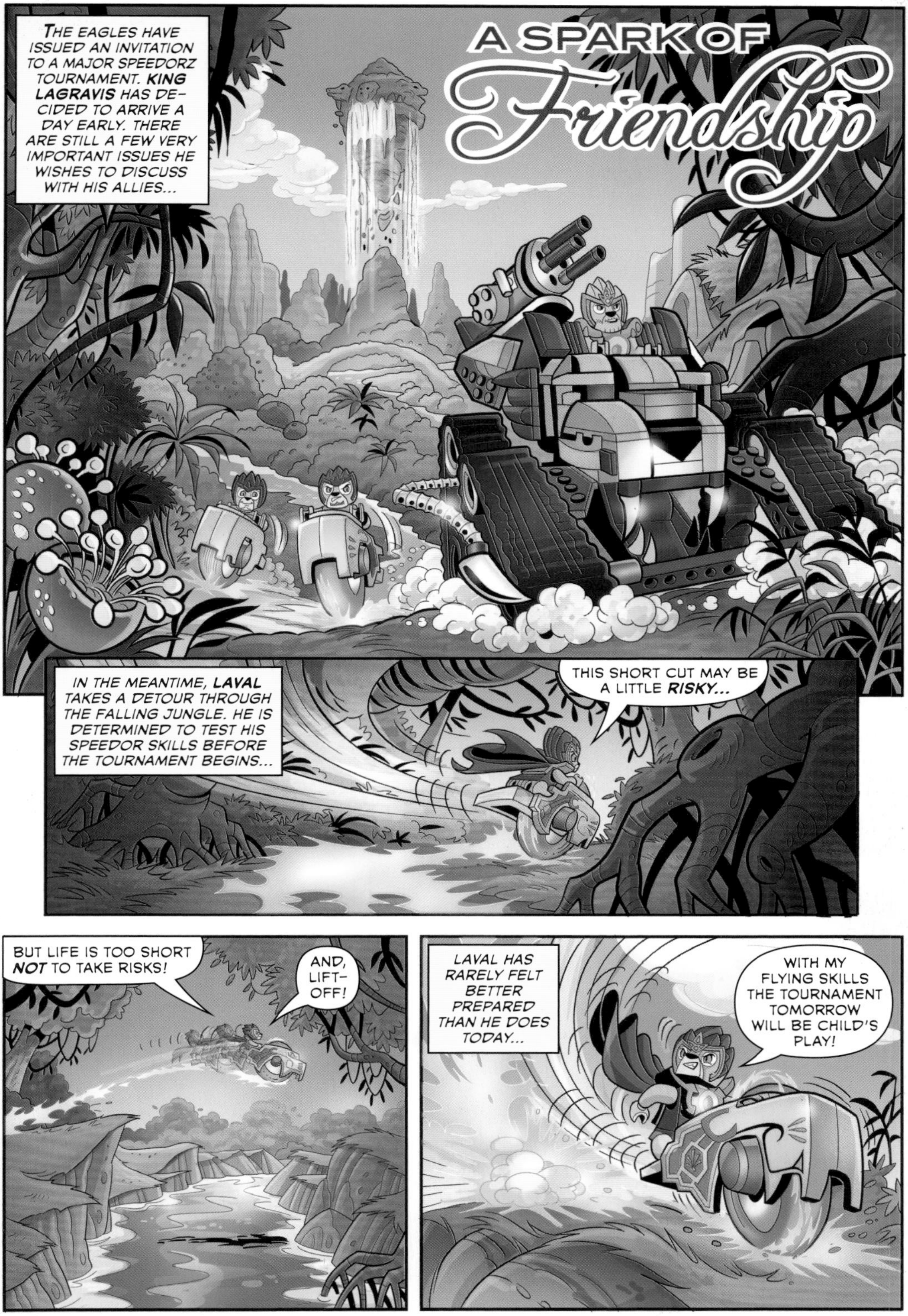
THE EAGLES HAVE ISSUED AN INVITATION TO A MAJOR SPEEDORZ TOURNAMENT. KING LAGRAVIS HAS DECIDED TO ARRIVE A DAY EARLY. THERE ARE STILL A FEW VERY IMPORTANT ISSUES HE WISHES TO DISCUSS WITH HIS ALLIES...
A SPARK OF Friendship
IN THE MEANTIME, LAVAL TAKES A DETOUR THROUGH THE FALLING JUNGLE. HE IS DETERMINED TO TEST HIS SPEEDOR SKILLS BEFORE THE TOURNAMENT BEGINS...
THIS SHORT CUT MAY BE A LITTLE RISKY...
BUT LIFE IS TOO SHORT NOT TO TAKE RISKS!
AND, LIFT-OFF!
LAVAL HAS RARELY FELT BETTER PREPARED THAN HE DOES TODAY...
WITH MY FLYING SKILLS THE TOURNAMENT TOMORROW WILL BE CHILD'S PLAY!

A FEW HOURS LATER, LAVAL HAS REACHED THE EAGLES' CASTLE...

HIS FATHER HAS ALSO ARRIVED.

HOW DID THEY GET HERE *BEFORE* ME?

LAGRAVIS. IT IS GOOD THAT YOU WERE ABLE TO COME EARLIER. WE CAN TALK IN PEACE WITHOUT THE CROCODILES EAVESDROPPING ON US.

WHAT? THE CROCODILES ARE COMING TOO?!

EWALD, THE LEADER OF THE EAGLES' RULING COUNCIL, WELCOMES THE LIONS. LAVAL IS APPALLED WHEN HE LEARNS WHO ELSE IS TAKING PART IN THE TOURNAMENT...

THEY WOULD ONLY CAUSE US MORE TROUBLE IF WE HADN'T INVITED THEM.

BUT OUR LAST TOURNAMENT HAD TO BE ABANDONED BECAUSE CRAGGER ATTACKED ERIS! BELIEVE ME, YOU DON'T WANT HIM AROUND!

LAVAL, PLEASE ACCEPT EWALD'S DECISION. IT IS THE EAGLES WHO ARE ORGANIZING THE TOURNAMENT. NOT US.

I DON'T BELIEVE IT!

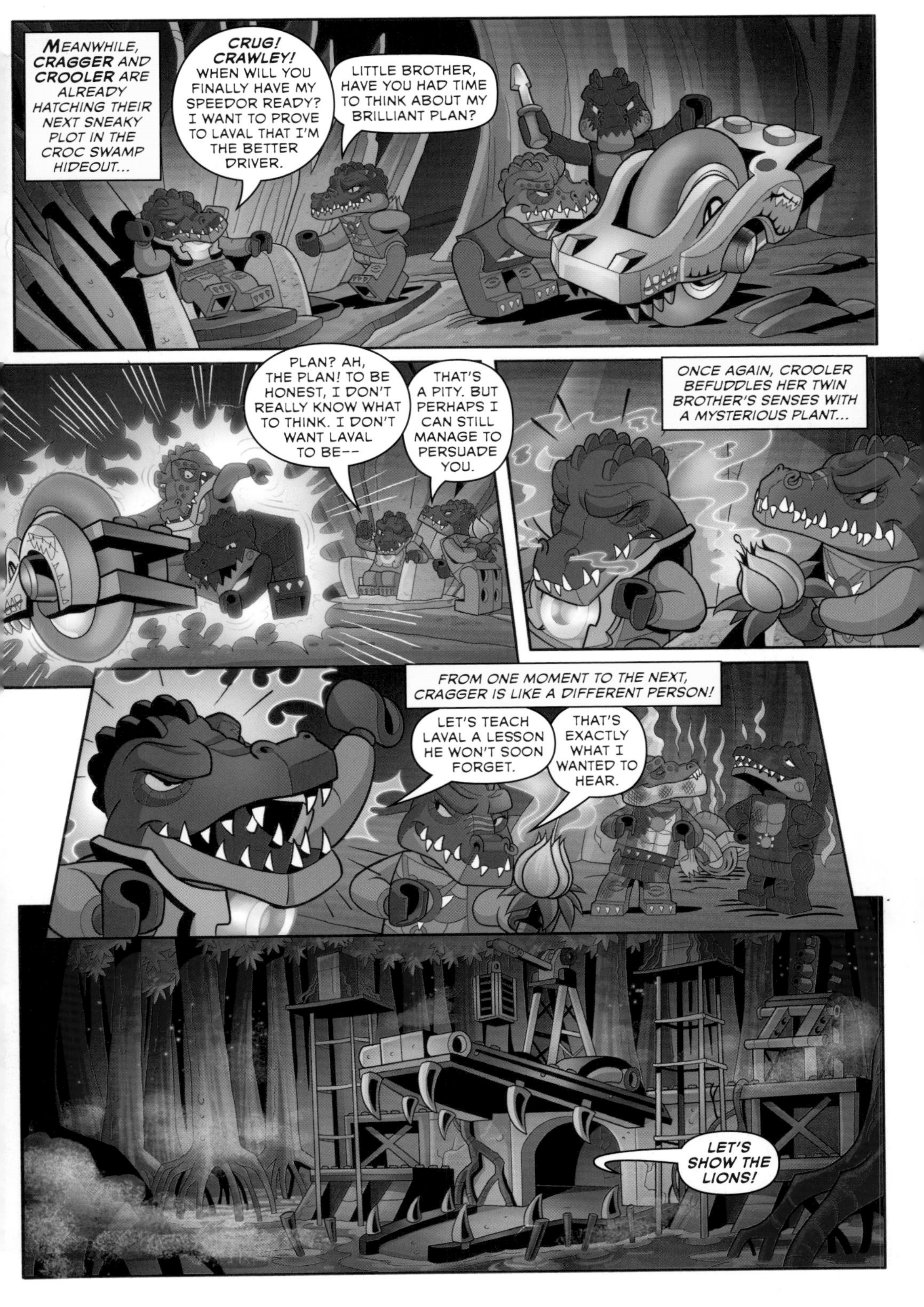
MEANWHILE, CRAGGER AND CROOLER ARE ALREADY HATCHING THEIR NEXT SNEAKY PLOT IN THE CROC SWAMP HIDEOUT...
CRUG! CRAWLEY! WHEN WILL YOU FINALLY HAVE MY SPEEDOR READY? I WANT TO PROVE TO LAVAL THAT I'M THE BETTER DRIVER.
LITTLE BROTHER, HAVE YOU HAD TIME TO THINK ABOUT MY BRILLIANT PLAN?
PLAN? AH, THE PLAN! TO BE HONEST, I DON'T REALLY KNOW WHAT TO THINK. I DON'T WANT LAVAL TO BE--
THAT'S A PITY. BUT PERHAPS I CAN STILL MANAGE TO PERSUADE YOU.
ONCE AGAIN, CROOLER BEFUDDLES HER TWIN BROTHER'S SENSES WITH A MYSTERIOUS PLANT...
FROM ONE MOMENT TO THE NEXT, CRAGGER IS LIKE A DIFFERENT PERSON!
LET'S TEACH LAVAL A LESSON HE WON'T SOON FORGET.
THAT'S EXACTLY WHAT I WANTED TO HEAR.
LET'S SHOW THE LIONS!

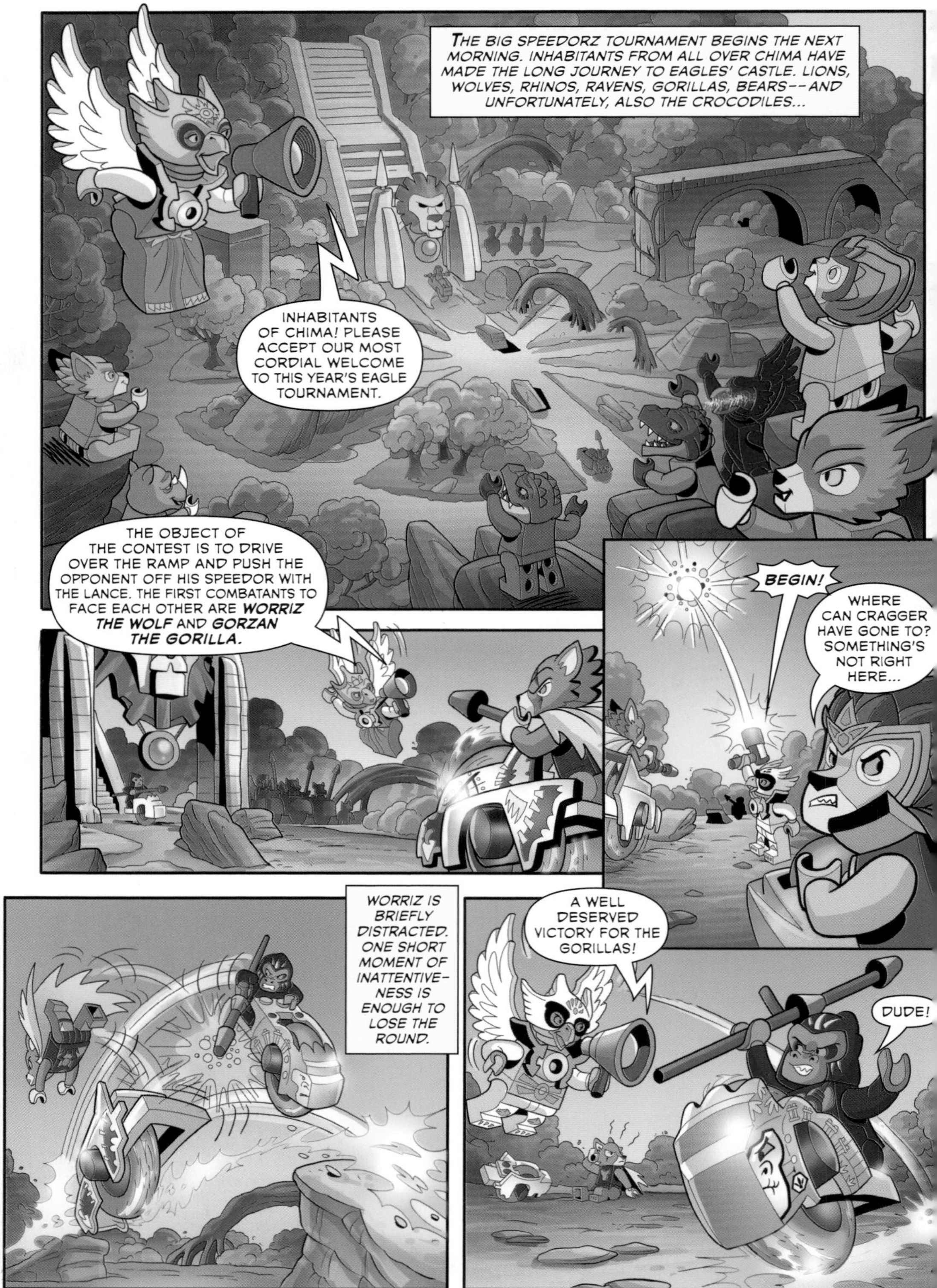
THE BIG SPEEDORZ TOURNAMENT BEGINS THE NEXT MORNING. INHABITANTS FROM ALL OVER CHIMA HAVE MADE THE LONG JOURNEY TO EAGLES' CASTLE. LIONS, WOLVES, RHINOS, RAVENS, GORILLAS, BEARS--AND UNFORTUNATELY, ALSO THE CROCODILES...
INHABITANTS OF CHIMA! PLEASE ACCEPT OUR MOST CORDIAL WELCOME TO THIS YEAR'S EAGLE TOURNAMENT.
THE OBJECT OF THE CONTEST IS TO DRIVE OVER THE RAMP AND PUSH THE OPPONENT OFF HIS SPEEDOR WITH THE LANCE. THE FIRST COMBATANTS TO FACE EACH OTHER ARE WORRIZ THE WOLF AND GORZAN THE GORILLA.
BEGIN!
WHERE CAN CRAGGER HAVE GONE TO? SOMETHING'S NOT RIGHT HERE...
WORRIZ IS BRIEFLY DISTRACTED. ONE SHORT MOMENT OF INATTENTIVE-NESS IS ENOUGH TO LOSE THE ROUND.
A WELL DESERVED VICTORY FOR THE GORILLAS!
DUDE!

21

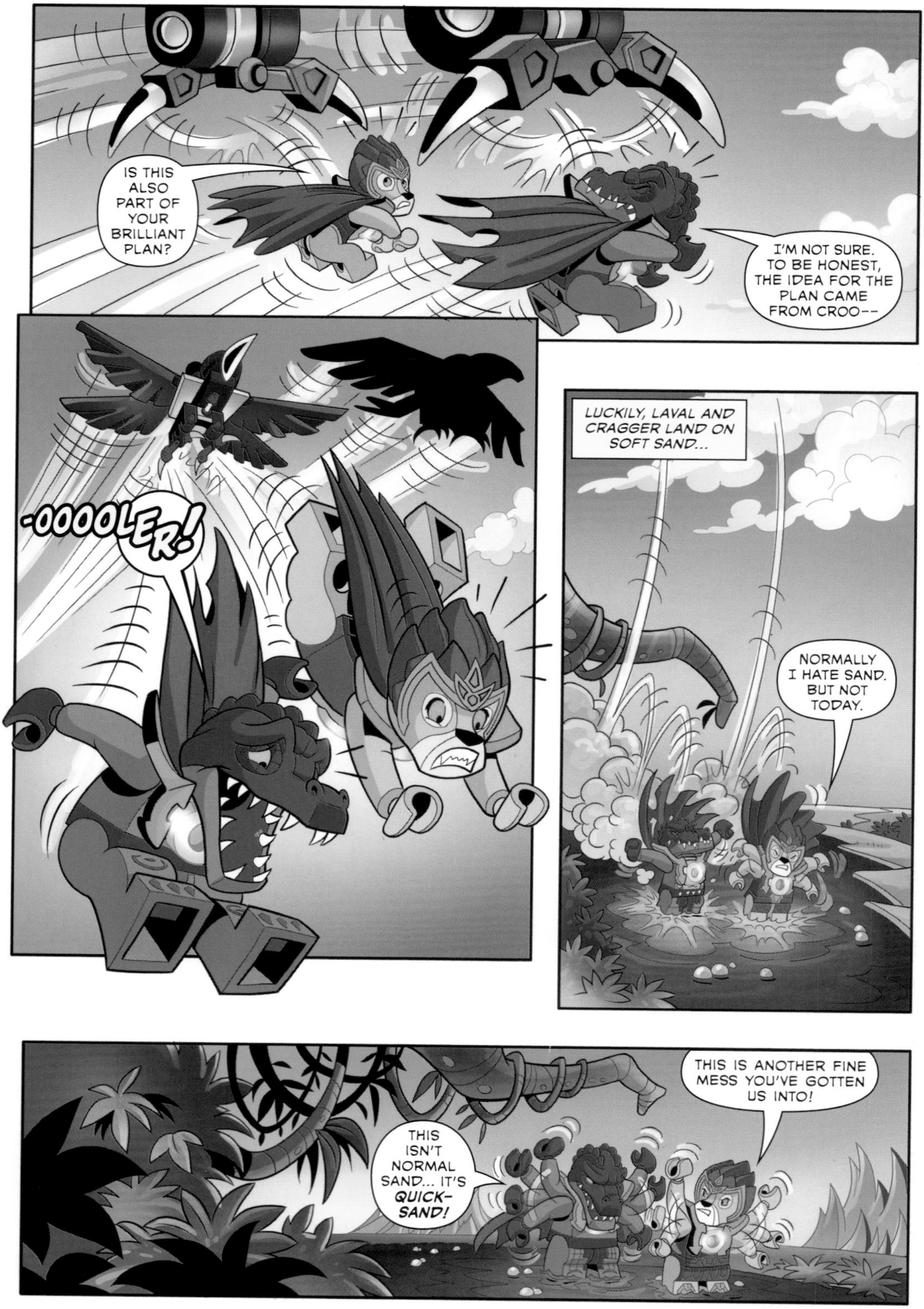

IS THIS ALSO PART OF YOUR BRILLIANT PLAN?
I'M NOT SURE. TO BE HONEST, THE IDEA FOR THE PLAN CAME FROM CROO--
-OOOOLER!
LUCKILY, LAVAL AND CRAGGER LAND ON SOFT SAND...
NORMALLY I HATE SAND. BUT NOT TODAY.
THIS IS ANOTHER FINE MESS YOU'VE GOTTEN US INTO!
THIS ISN'T NORMAL SAND... IT'S QUICK-SAND!

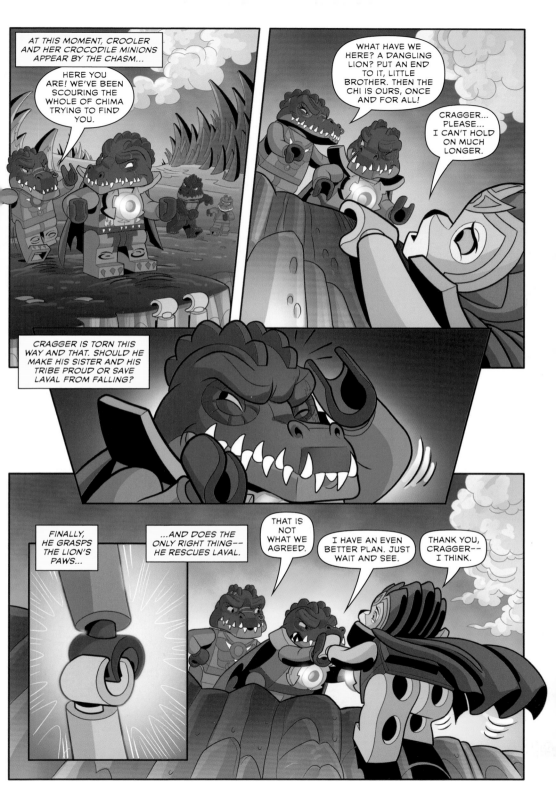

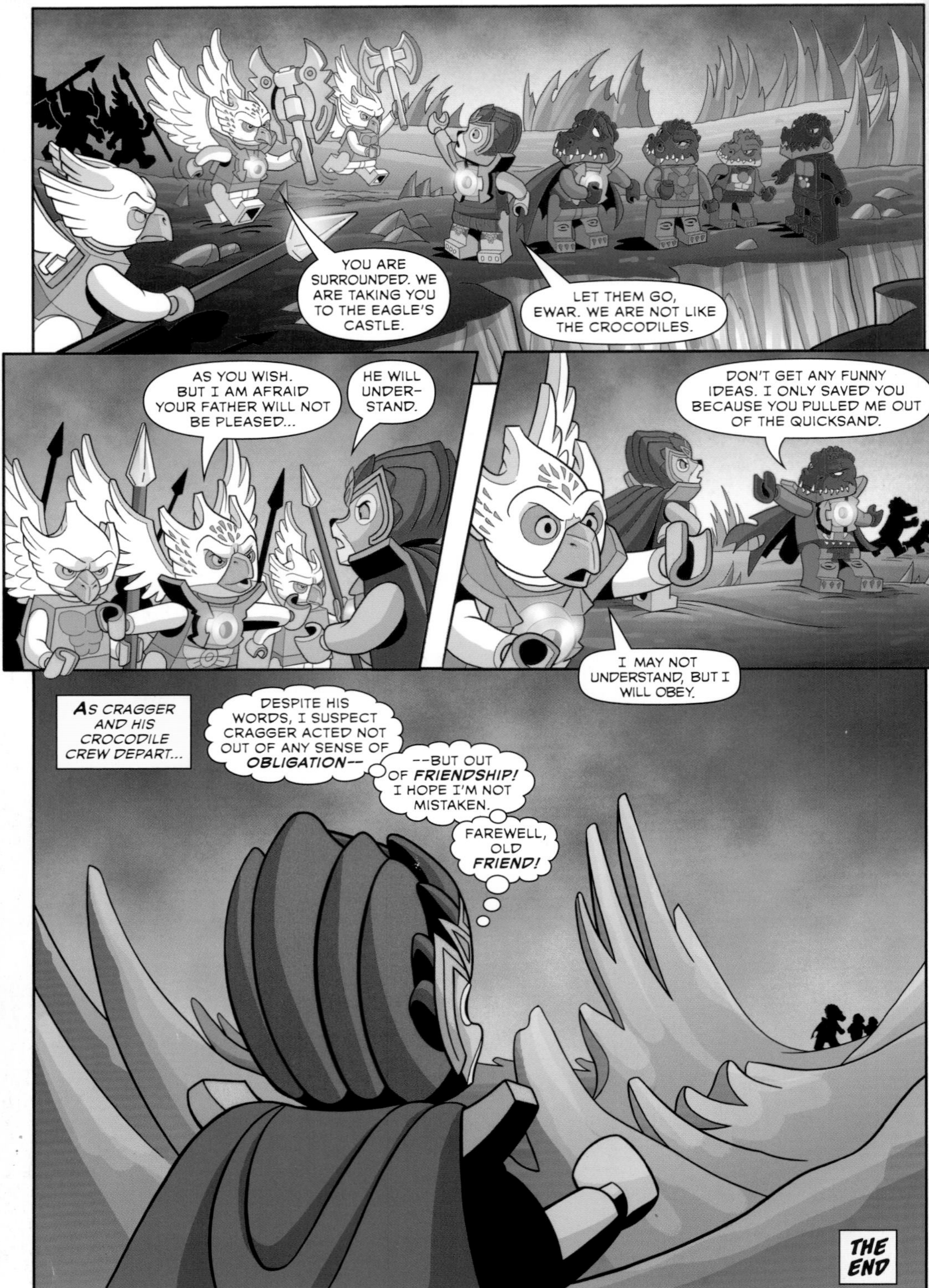

YOU ARE SURROUNDED. WE ARE TAKING YOU TO THE EAGLE'S CASTLE.
LET THEM GO, EWAR. WE ARE NOT LIKE THE CROCODILES.
AS YOU WISH. BUT I AM AFRAID YOUR FATHER WILL NOT BE PLEASED...
HE WILL UNDER-STAND.
DON'T GET ANY FUNNY IDEAS. I ONLY SAVED YOU BECAUSE YOU PULLED ME OUT OF THE QUICKSAND.
I MAY NOT UNDERSTAND, BUT I WILL OBEY.
AS CRAGGER AND HIS CROCODILE CREW DEPART...
DESPITE HIS WORDS, I SUSPECT CRAGGER ACTED NOT OUT OF ANY SENSE OF OBLIGATION--
--BUT OUT OF FRIENDSHIP! I HOPE I'M NOT MISTAKEN.
FAREWELL, OLD FRIEND!
THE END

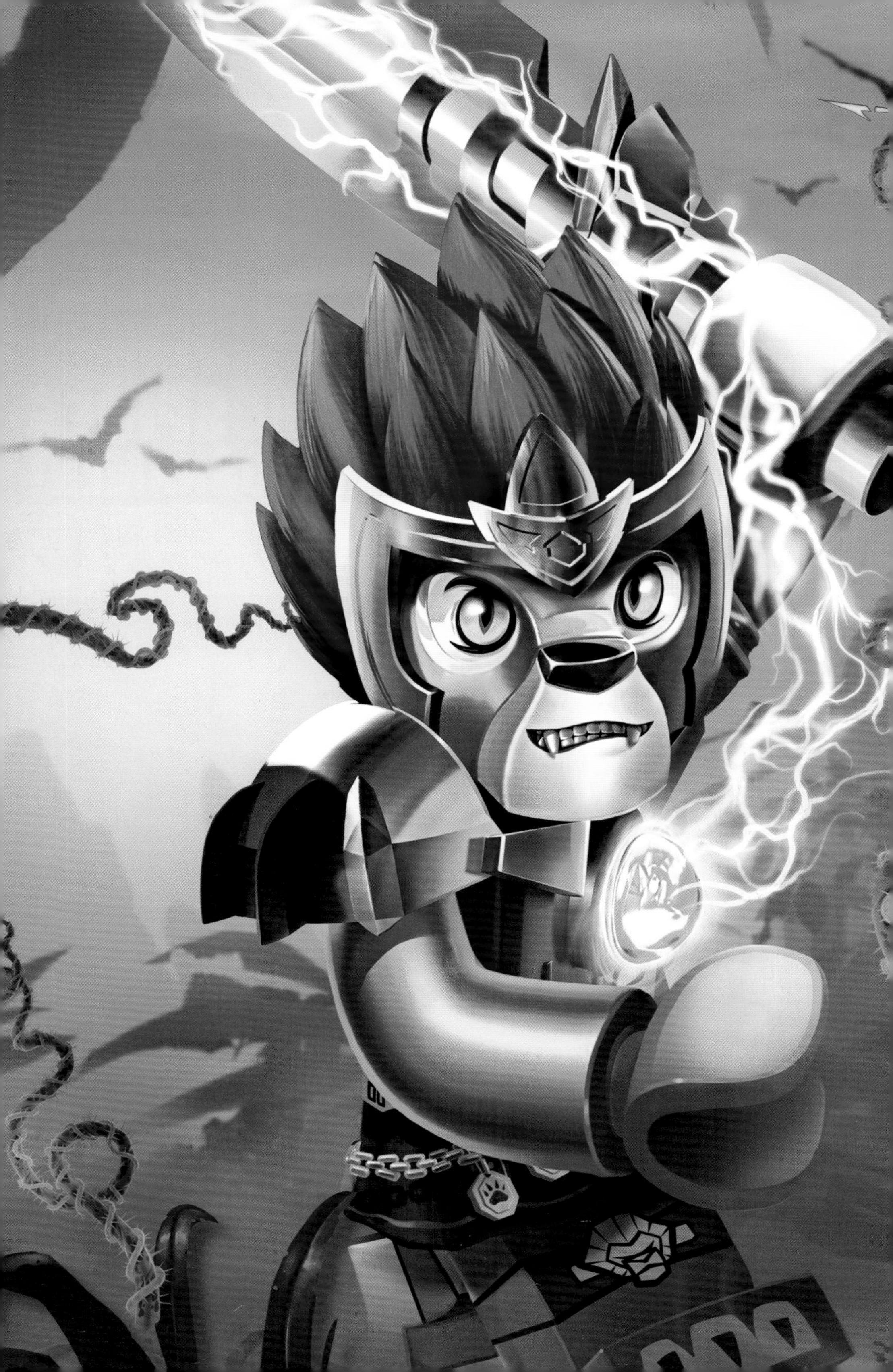

31

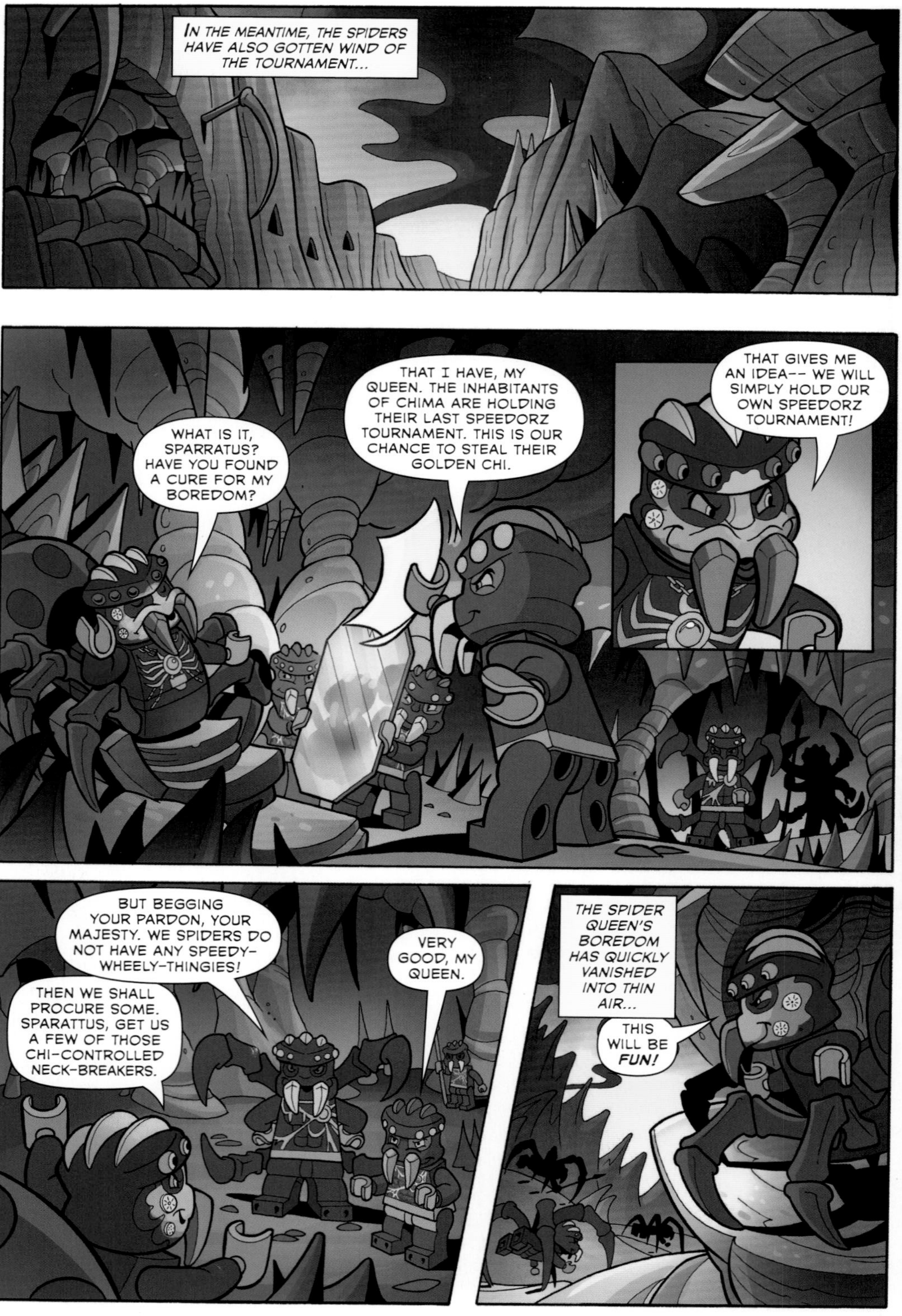
IN THE MEANTIME, THE SPIDERS HAVE ALSO GOTTEN WIND OF THE TOURNAMENT...
WHAT IS IT, SPARRATUS? HAVE YOU FOUND A CURE FOR MY BOREDOM?
THAT I HAVE, MY QUEEN. THE INHABITANTS OF CHIMA ARE HOLDING THEIR LAST SPEEDORZ TOURNAMENT. THIS IS OUR CHANCE TO STEAL THEIR GOLDEN CHI.
THAT GIVES ME AN IDEA-- WE WILL SIMPLY HOLD OUR OWN SPEEDORZ TOURNAMENT!
BUT BEGGING YOUR PARDON, YOUR MAJESTY. WE SPIDERS DO NOT HAVE ANY SPEEDY-WHEELY-THINGIES!
THEN WE SHALL PROCURE SOME. SPARATTUS, GET US A FEW OF THOSE CHI-CONTROLLED NECK-BREAKERS.
VERY GOOD, MY QUEEN.
THE SPIDER QUEEN'S BOREDOM HAS QUICKLY VANISHED INTO THIN AIR...
THIS WILL BE *FUN!*

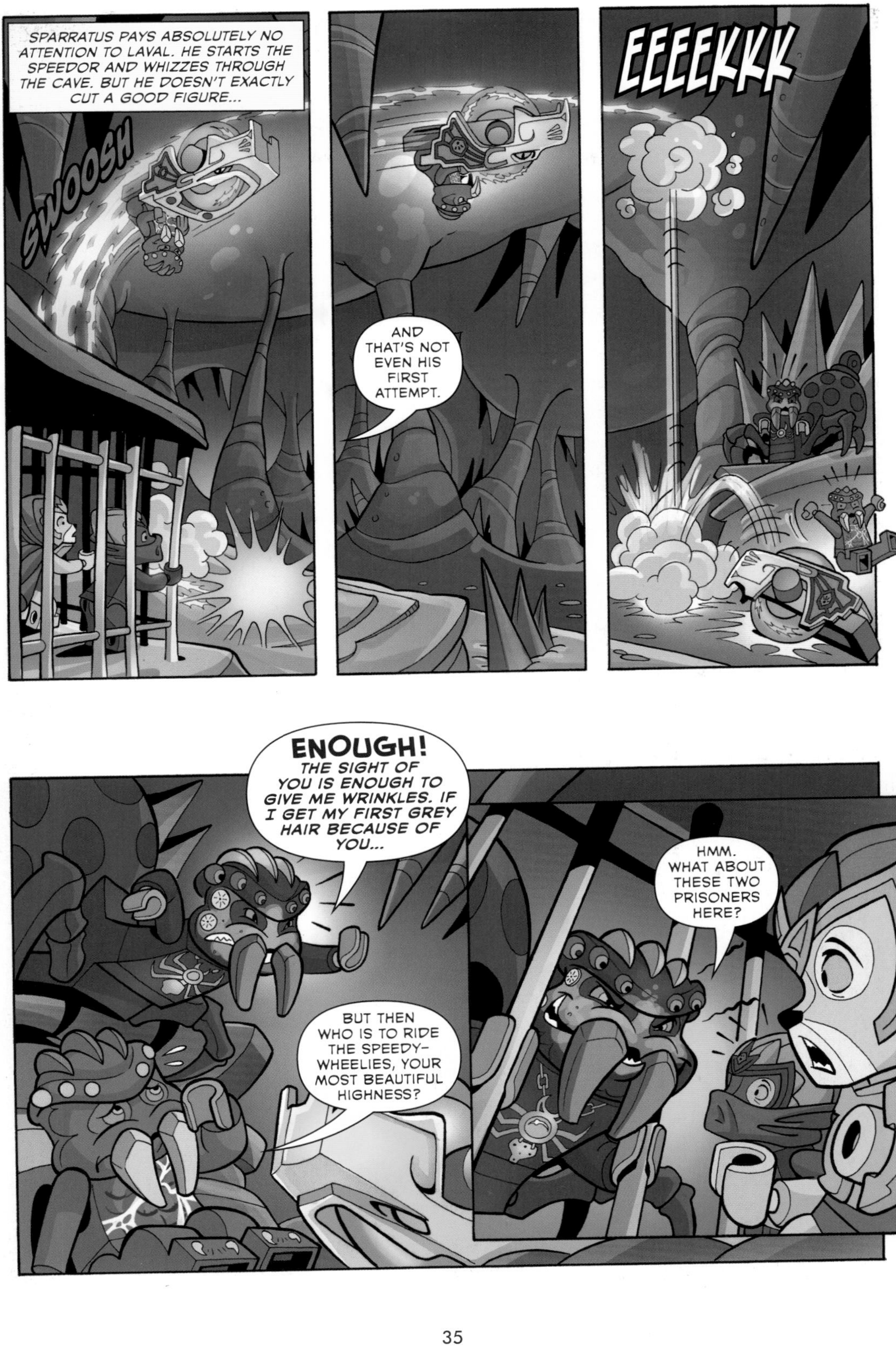
SPARRATUS PAYS ABSOLUTELY NO ATTENTION TO LAVAL. HE STARTS THE SPEEDOR AND WHIZZES THROUGH THE CAVE. BUT HE DOESN'T EXACTLY CUT A GOOD FIGURE...
SWOOSH
AND THAT'S NOT EVEN HIS FIRST ATTEMPT.
EEEEKKK
ENOUGH! THE SIGHT OF YOU IS ENOUGH TO GIVE ME WRINKLES. IF I GET MY FIRST GREY HAIR BECAUSE OF YOU...
BUT THEN WHO IS TO RIDE THE SPEEDY-WHEELIES, YOUR MOST BEAUTIFUL HIGHNESS?
HMM. WHAT ABOUT THESE TWO PRISONERS HERE?

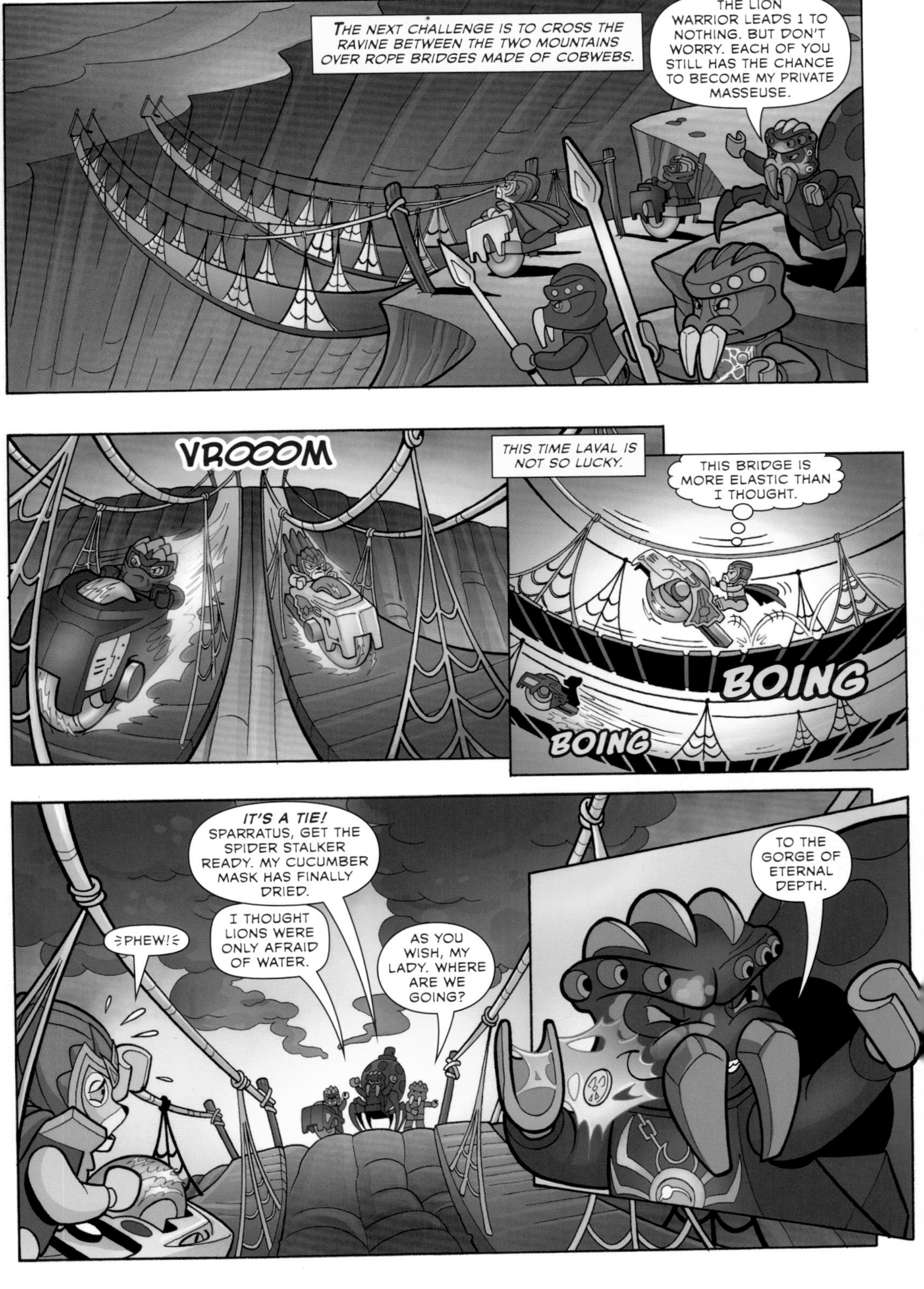
THE NEXT CHALLENGE IS TO CROSS THE RAVINE BETWEEN THE TWO MOUNTAINS OVER ROPE BRIDGES MADE OF COBWEBS.
THE LION WARRIOR LEADS 1 TO NOTHING. BUT DON'T WORRY. EACH OF YOU STILL HAS THE CHANCE TO BECOME MY PRIVATE MASSEUSE.
VROOOM
THIS TIME LAVAL IS NOT SO LUCKY.
THIS BRIDGE IS MORE ELASTIC THAN I THOUGHT.
BOING
BOING
IT'S A TIE! SPARRATUS, GET THE SPIDER STALKER READY. MY CUCUMBER MASK HAS FINALLY DRIED.
PHEW!
I THOUGHT LIONS WERE ONLY AFRAID OF WATER.
AS YOU WISH, MY LADY. WHERE ARE WE GOING?
TO THE GORGE OF ETERNAL DEPTH.

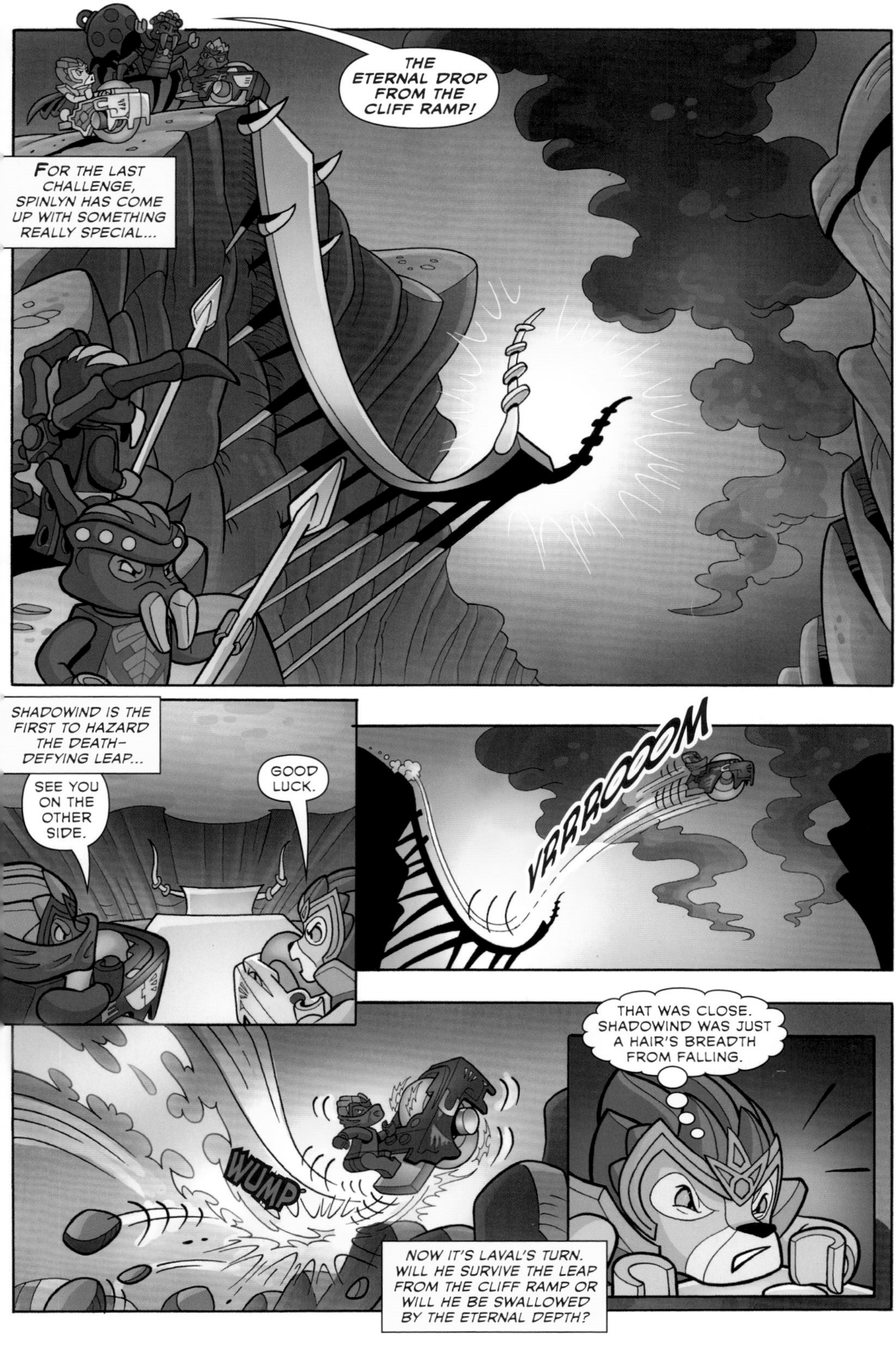
THE ETERNAL DROP FROM THE CLIFF RAMP!
FOR THE LAST CHALLENGE, SPINLYN HAS COME UP WITH SOMETHING REALLY SPECIAL...
SHADOWIND IS THE FIRST TO HAZARD THE DEATH-DEFYING LEAP...
SEE YOU ON THE OTHER SIDE.
GOOD LUCK.
VRRROOOM
WUMP
THAT WAS CLOSE. SHADOWIND WAS JUST A HAIR'S BREADTH FROM FALLING.
NOW IT'S LAVAL'S TURN. WILL HE SURVIVE THE LEAP FROM THE CLIFF RAMP OR WILL HE BE SWALLOWED BY THE ETERNAL DEPTH?

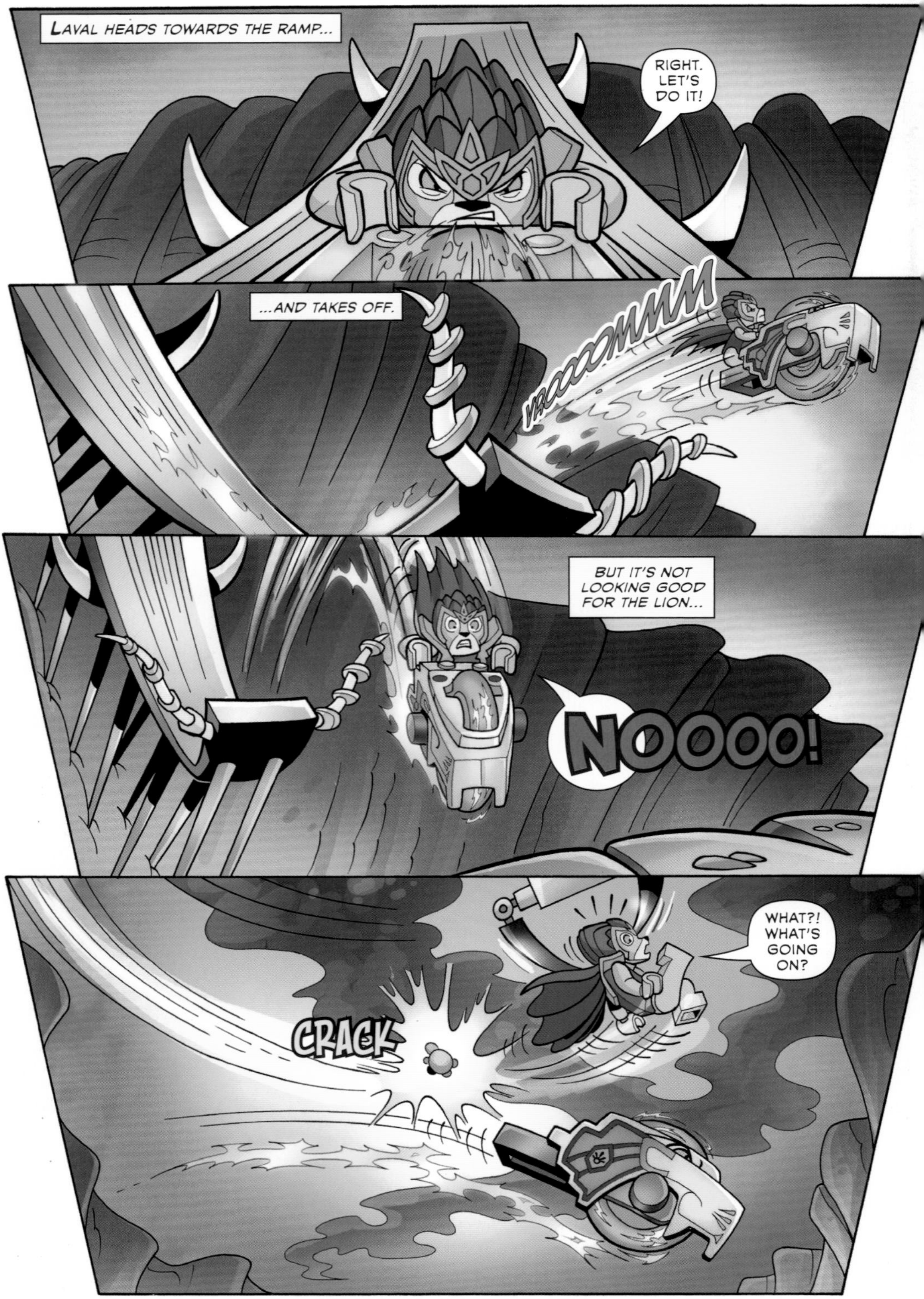
LAVAL HEADS TOWARDS THE RAMP...
RIGHT. LET'S DO IT!
...AND TAKES OFF.
VROOOOOMMMM
BUT IT'S NOT LOOKING GOOD FOR THE LION...
NOOOO!
WHAT?! WHAT'S GOING ON?
CRACK

41

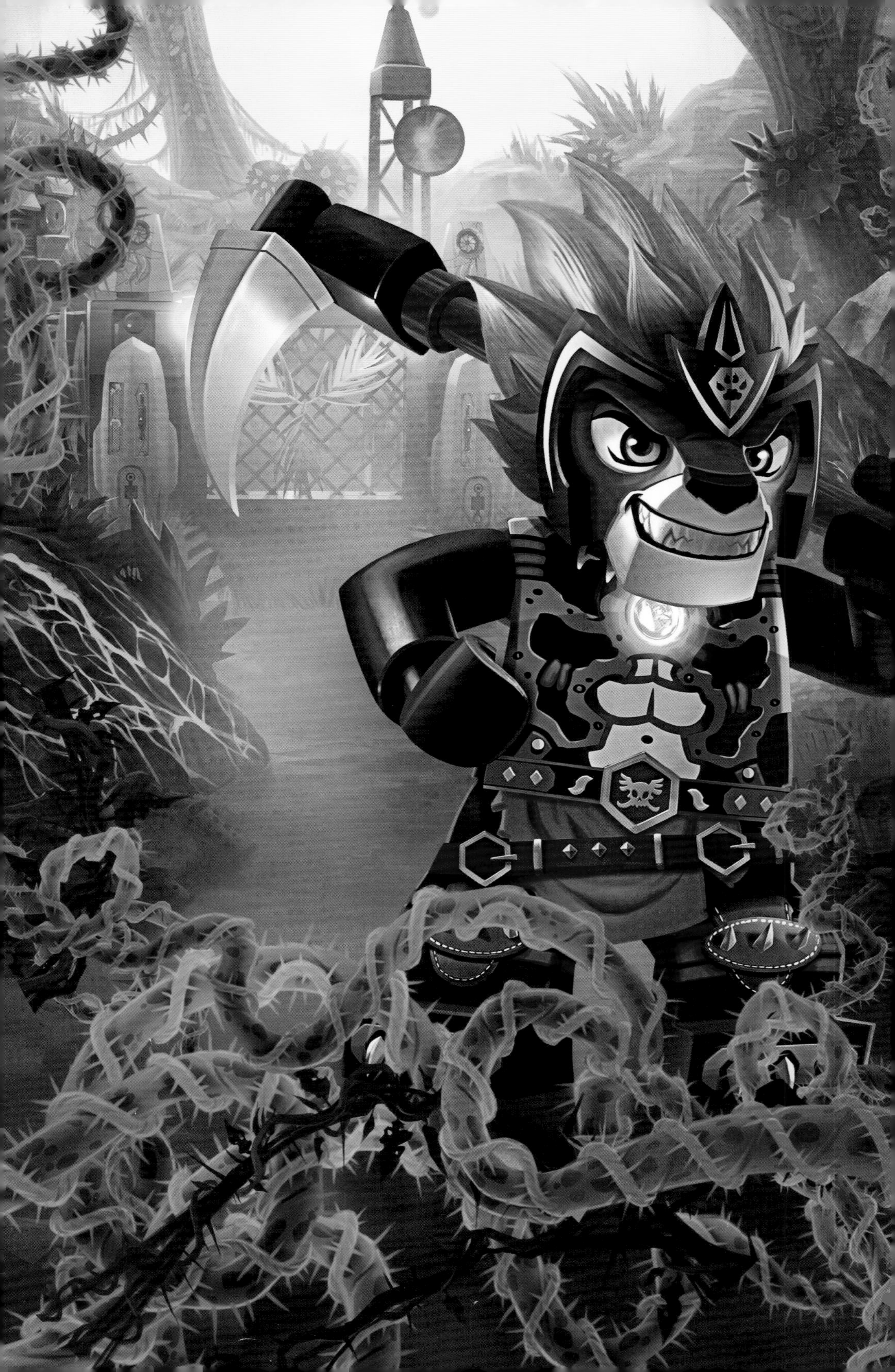

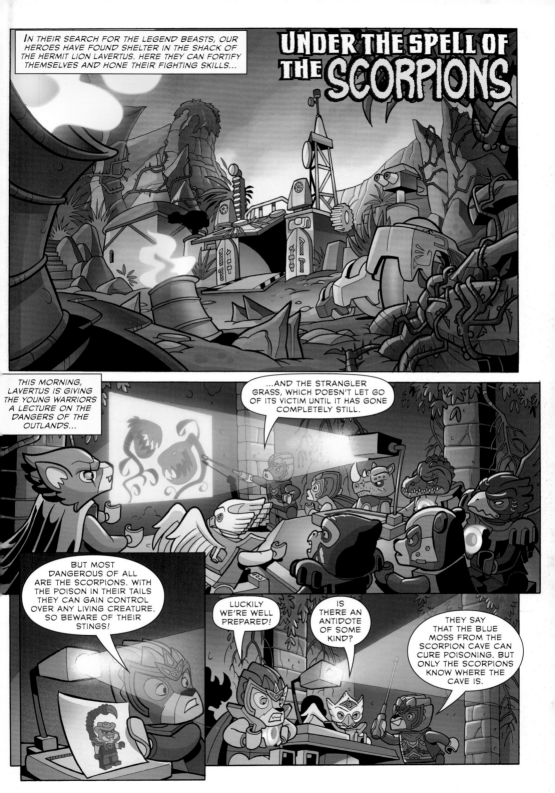

44

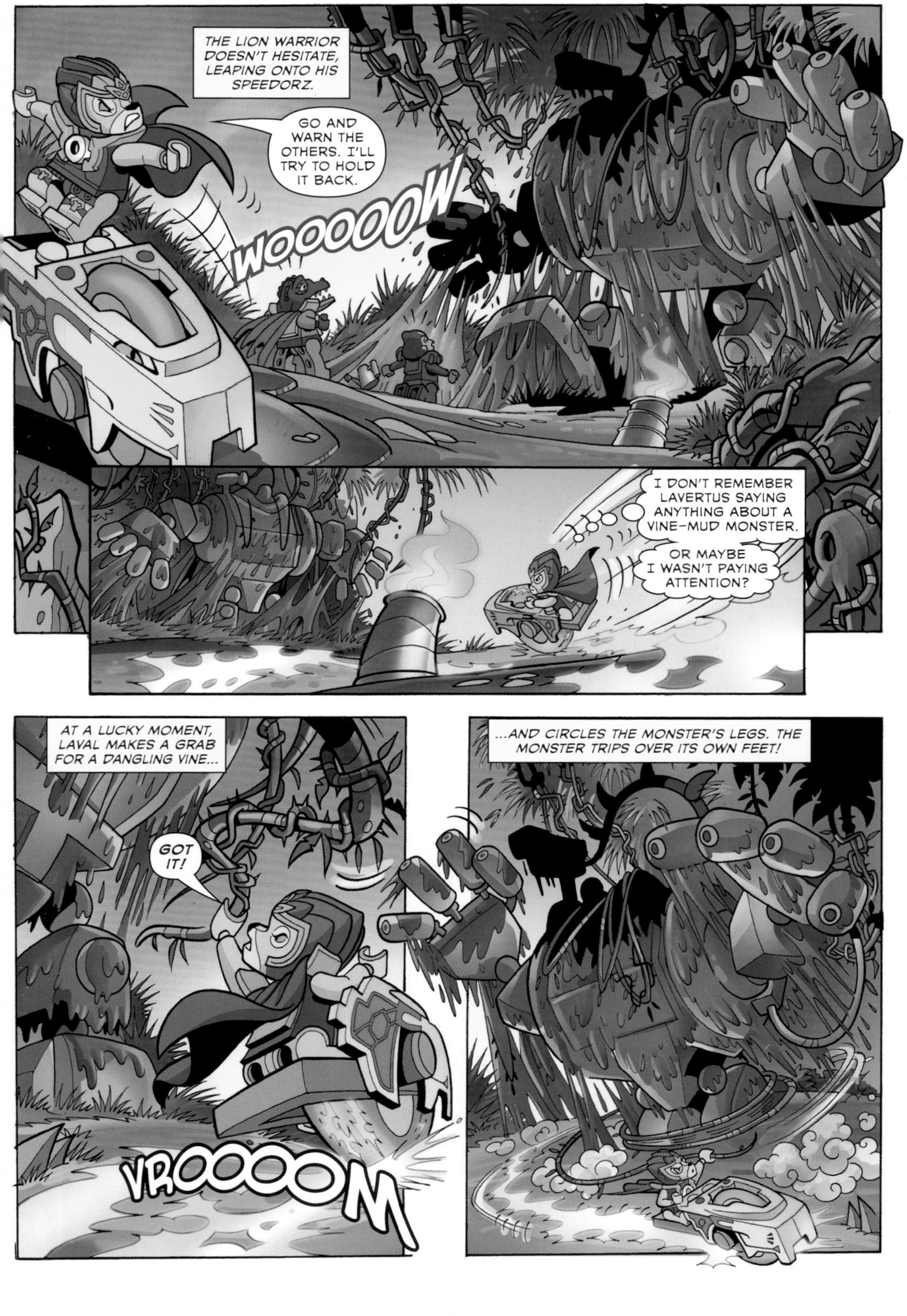
THE LION WARRIOR DOESN'T HESITATE, LEAPING ONTO HIS SPEEDORZ.
GO AND WARN THE OTHERS. I'LL TRY TO HOLD IT BACK.
WOOOOOW
I DON'T REMEMBER LAVERTUS SAYING ANYTHING ABOUT A VINE-MUD MONSTER.
OR MAYBE I WASN'T PAYING ATTENTION?
AT A LUCKY MOMENT, LAVAL MAKES A GRAB FOR A DANGLING VINE...
GOT IT!
VROOOOM
...AND CIRCLES THE MONSTER'S LEGS. THE MONSTER TRIPS OVER ITS OWN FEET!

47

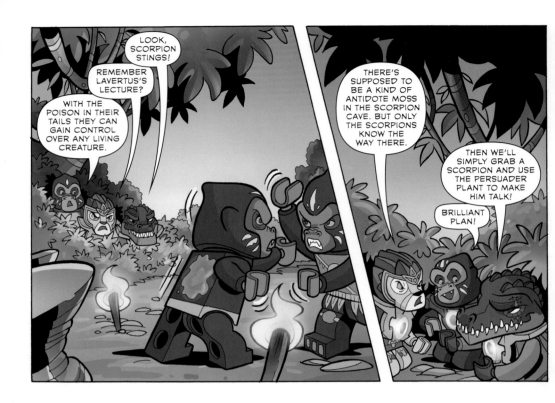

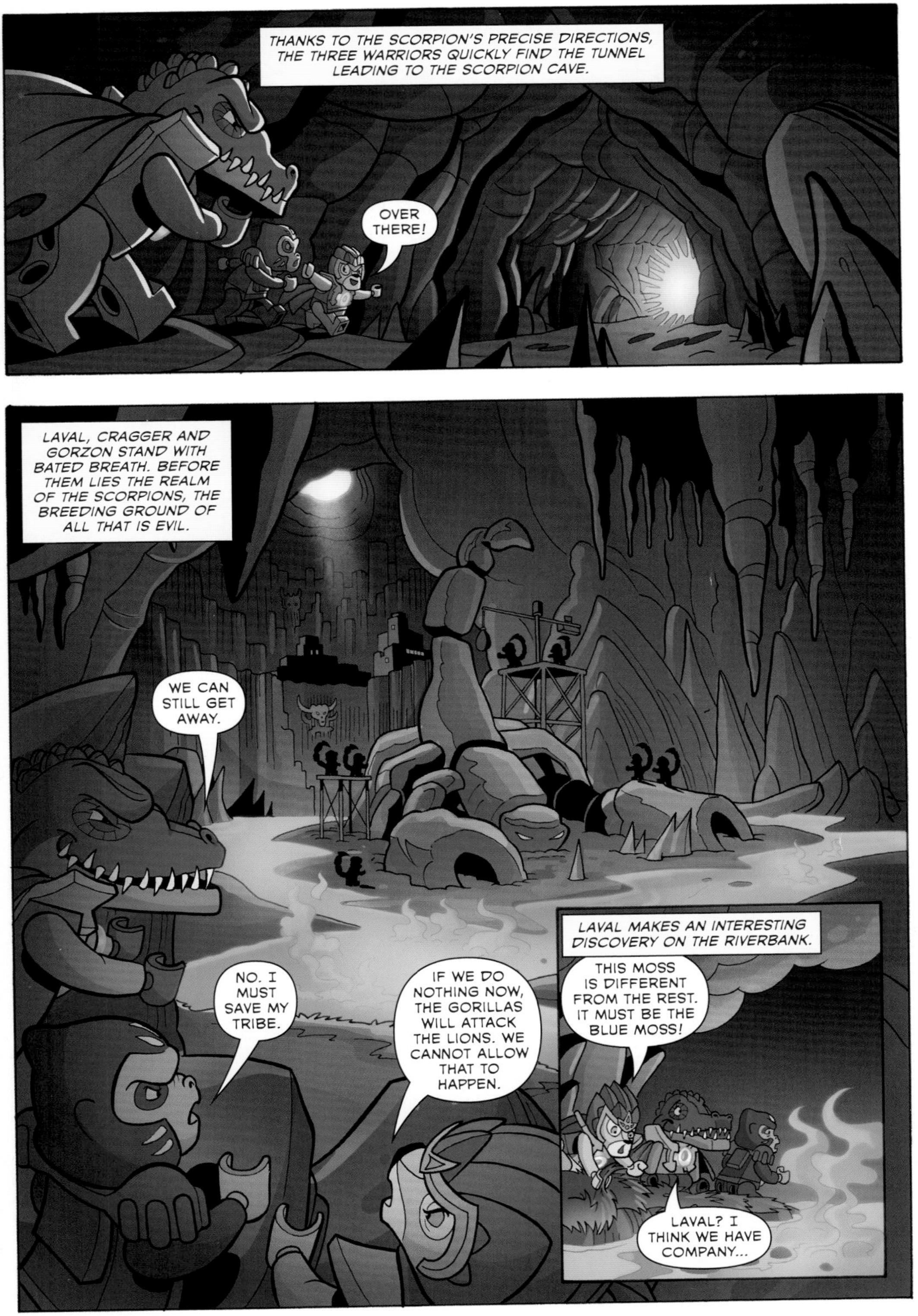
THANKS TO THE SCORPION'S PRECISE DIRECTIONS, THE THREE WARRIORS QUICKLY FIND THE TUNNEL LEADING TO THE SCORPION CAVE.
OVER THERE!
LAVAL, CRAGGER AND GORZON STAND WITH BATED BREATH. BEFORE THEM LIES THE REALM OF THE SCORPIONS, THE BREEDING GROUND OF ALL THAT IS EVIL.
WE CAN STILL GET AWAY.
NO. I MUST SAVE MY TRIBE.
IF WE DO NOTHING NOW, THE GORILLAS WILL ATTACK THE LIONS. WE CANNOT ALLOW THAT TO HAPPEN.
LAVAL MAKES AN INTERESTING DISCOVERY ON THE RIVERBANK.
THIS MOSS IS DIFFERENT FROM THE REST. IT MUST BE THE BLUE MOSS!
LAVAL? I THINK WE HAVE COMPANY...

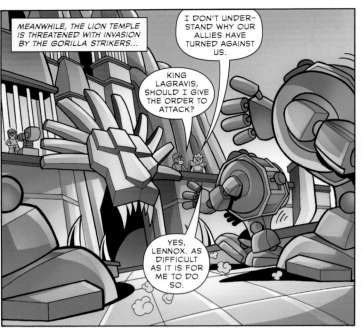

MEANWHILE, THE LION TEMPLE IS THREATENED WITH INVASION BY THE GORILLA STRIKERS...

I DON'T UNDER-STAND WHY OUR ALLIES HAVE TURNED AGAINST US.

KING LAGRAVIS, SHOULD I GIVE THE ORDER TO ATTACK?

YES, LENNOX. AS DIFFICULT AS IT IS FOR ME TO DO SO.

I DON'T BELIEVE MY EYES. IS THAT LAVAL STANDING DOWN THERE ON THE BRIDGE?!

STOP! HOLD YOUR FIRE!

ARE YOU READY?

READIER THAN READY!

ALL THREE USE A CHI ORB.

FOR CHIMA!

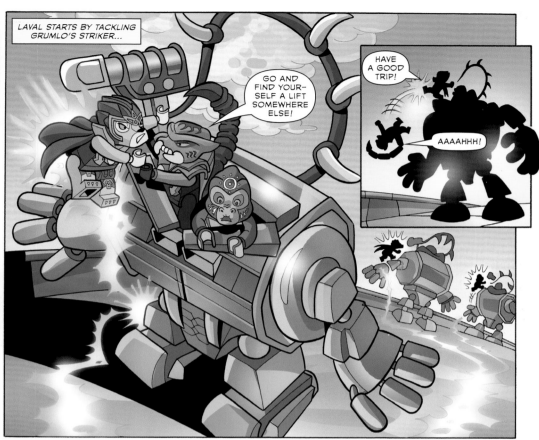

LAVAL STARTS BY TACKLING GRUMLO'S STRIKER...

GO AND FIND YOURSELF A LIFT SOMEWHERE ELSE!

HAVE A GOOD TRIP!

AAAAHHH!

EVEN AS GRUMLO IS CHEWING, THE ANTIDOTE MOSS STARTS TO TAKE EFFECT. THE FIRST POISONING HAS BEEN CURED!

WHAT... WHAT HAPPENED?

THE SCORPIONS POISONED YOU AND HAVE TAKEN OVER THE OTHER GORILLAS' MINDS. BUT DON'T WORRY, WE'RE GOING TO RESCUE THEM AS WELL.

EAT THIS, GORILLA!

THE GORILLA WASN'T EXPECTING THAT.

WATCH OUT FOR PAPERCUTZ

Welcome to the Chi-filled first LEGO® LEGENDS OF CHIMA graphic novel, by Yannick Grotholt and Comicon, from Papercutz, the animal-loving folks dedicated to publishing great graphic novels for all ages.

As I write these words, the recently released THE LEGO MOVIE is breaking all sorts of box office records as the #1 movie in North America. But even more exciting for us on a personal level, our LEGO NINJAGO #9 "Night of the Nindroids" is the #1 graphic book (paperback) on The New York Times best-seller list! And we can't think of any better way to celebrate LEGO's super-success than by publishing LEGO LEGENDS OF CHIMA—the graphic novel series you've been demanding to see!

Clearly, this is a great time to be a LEGO fan! But it keeps getting better! LEGO NINJAGO is back on Cartoon Network with several all-new specials, and LEGO LEGENDS OF CHIMA is also a huge hit on Cartoon Network! The excitement just doesn't seem to end!

And speaking of exciting, we've been meaning to mention for some time that our LEGO NINJAGO graphic novels are also published in Germany, as part of a LEGO NINJAGO magazine published by our friends at Blue Ocean. Now, our roles are reversed and we're publishing comics originally published first in the LEGO LEGENDS OF CHIMA comics magazine in Germany—translated into English, of course! So rather than getting one great big story like we usually present in LEGO NINJAGO, we're getting four stories from four issues of their magazine to publish in one of our graphic novels.

One of the interesting differences between a magazine and a graphic novel, is that Papercutz fans have come to expect complete stories in our books. The folks at Blue Ocean did something rather interesting with the ending of the "A Spark of Friendship" story—they added a cliff-hanger ending and asked LEGO fans to send in their ideas of how that story would end. We thought that might be a little bit confusing, so we brought in LEGO NINJAGO artist, Jolyon Yates, and colorist, Laurie E. Smith, to create a new last panel that more clearly concludes the story. But just for fun, here's a look at the original last two panels:

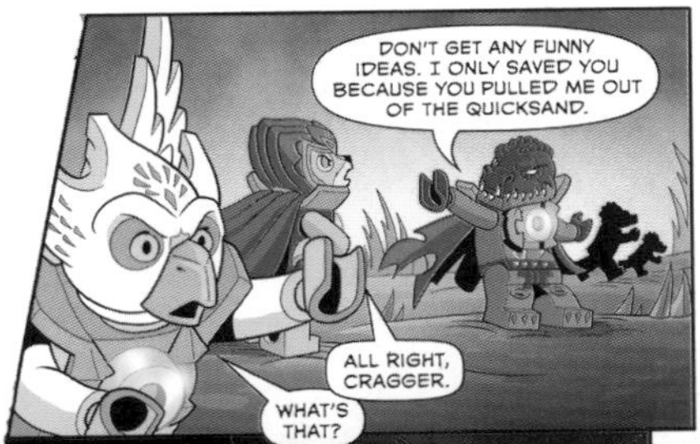
DON'T GET ANY FUNNY IDEAS. I ONLY SAVED YOU BECAUSE YOU PULLED ME OUT OF THE QUICKSAND.
ALL RIGHT, CRAGGER.
WHAT'S THAT?

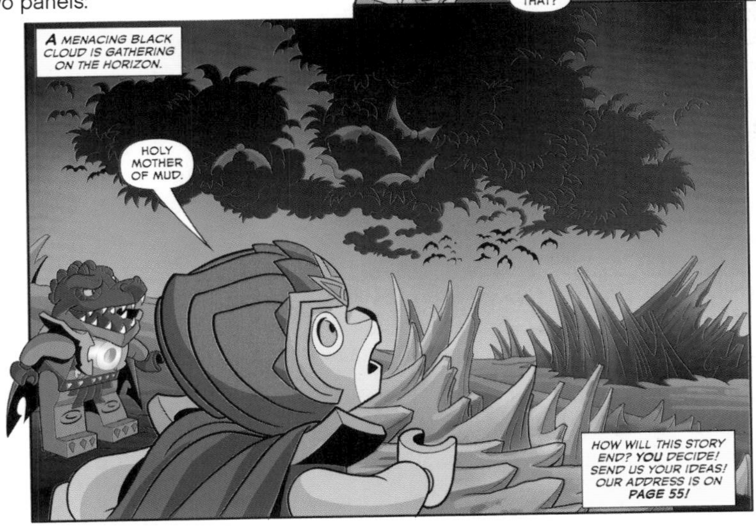
A MENACING BLACK CLOUD IS GATHERING ON THE HORIZON.
HOLY MOTHER OF MUD.
HOW WILL THIS STORY END? YOU DECIDE! SEND US YOUR IDEAS! OUR ADDRESS IS ON PAGE 55!

So, for the would-be-writers out there, here's your opportunity to tell us what you think happens next! Just send your ideas, scripts, etc., to the addresses listed below. We may showcase some of the best ones in a future LEGO LEGENDS OF CHIMA graphic novel.

In the meantime, keep an eye out for LEGO LEGENDS OF CHIMA #2 "The Right Decision" comic soon!

Long Live LEGO!

Thanks,

Jim

STAY IN TOUCH!

EMAIL:	salicrup@papercutz.com
WEB:	papercutz.com
TWITTER:	@papercutzgn
FACEBOOK:	PAPERCUTZGRAPHICNOVELS
FAN MAIL:	Papercutz, 160 Broadway, Suite 700, East Wing, New York, NY 10038

LEGO® GRAPHIC NOVELS AVAILABLE FROM PAPERCUTZ™

LEGO NINJAGO #1

LEGO NINJAGO #2

LEGO NINJAGO #3

LEGO NINJAGO #4

LEGO NINJAGO #5

LEGO NINJAGO #6

LEGO NINJAGO #7

LEGO NINJAGO #8

SPECIAL EDITION #1 (Features stories from NINJAGO #1 & #2.)

SPECIAL EDITION #2 (Features stories from NINJAGO #3 & #4.)

SPECIAL EDITION #3 (Features stories from NINJAGO #5 & #6.)

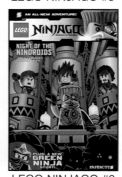
LEGO NINJAGO #9

LEGO® NINJAGO graphic novels are available in paperback and hardcover at booksellers everywhere.

LEGO® NINJAGO #1-10 are $6.99 in paperback, and $10.99 in hardcover. LEGO NINJAGO SPECIAL EDITION #1-3 are $10.99 in paperback only. You can also order online at papercutz.com. Or call 1-800-886-1223, Monday through Friday, 9 – 5 EST. MC, Visa, and AmEx accepted. To order by mail, please add $4.00 for postage and handling for first book ordered, $1.00 for each additional book and make check payable to NBM Publishing. Send to: Papercutz, 160 Broadway, Suite 700, East Wing, New York, NY 10038.

LEGO NINJAGO graphic novels are also available digitally wherever e-books are sold.

COMING SOON!

LEGO NINJAGO #10

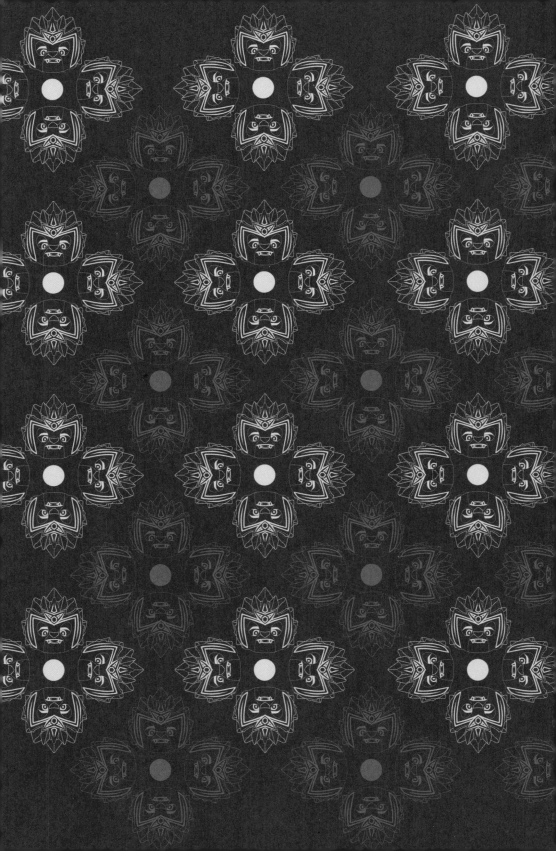